I0823211

Other Books by Marty Eberhardt

Bea Rivers Mystery Series

Death in a Desert Garden

Bones in the Back Forty

A Bea Rivers Mystery

by

Marty Eberhardt

Artemesia
Publishing

ISBN: 9781963832433 (paperback) / 9781963832648 (ebook)
LCCN: 2025950750

Printed in the United States of America.

Artemesia Publishing
9 Mockingbird Hill Rd
Tijeras, New Mexico 87059
info@artemesiapublishing.com
www.apbooks.net

For deserts and oceans.

CHAPTER ONE

It was April in Tucson, the "yellow month," people called it, because all over town, the bright-green-barked palo verde trees exploded with lemon-yellow blooms. As Bea drove to work, a breeze blew the delicate blossoms onto her windshield. The whole town was a botanical garden now, with the green-and-yellow trees punctuated by the spiky red flowers of ocotillos, at the tips of thorny branches that rose as much as twenty feet from the ground.

Bea pulled into Shandley Gardens, where she was the executive director. Even though she'd had three years to get used to the title, she had to laugh a little at its pompousness. Mostly she enjoyed her job, except when it swamped her personal life, as was always the case in spring. The flip side of spring beauty in the desert was that public gardens had to attract as many people as they could before summer temperatures crashed visitor numbers. But the spring special events season would soon be winding up, she reminded herself. Meanwhile, in the parking lot alone she was greeted by the pinkish-purple orchid-like flowers of the desert willows and the reds and oranges of the long-tubed flowers of hummingbird bushes. She headed into the cactus garden to check who'd opened their blooms since the day before. Sure enough, the hedgehog cacti had nearly eclipsed their spiny stems with magenta blossoms. Bea had half a mind to get back into her car and head out to the desert for a long hike.

But of course, this would not be possible. She opened

the door to her office, plopped down into her chair, and turned to her computer. The phone rang with an unfamiliar number. She let it go through to voice mail, but heard, "Bea, it's Paige Pearson."

Paige Pearson. Bea had known her years ago, at UC Santa Cruz, where they'd been undergrads. They'd met again at a recent botanical garden conference... Paige, too, had become an executive director. Bea picked up the phone as Paige was saying something about getting together.

"Hey, Paige."

"Oh good, you're there. Bea, how's it going over there in the desert?"

"Lots of flowers and lots of people. How's it going at that garden overlooking the ocean?"

"Challenging. So Bea, I'll come right to it. How would you feel about a weekend at the beach?"

"I always want to go to the beach. Especially around June or so, when it's a furnace here, and blessedly cool and cloudy out there..."

"I was thinking about in two weeks."

"Oh." *I don't know Paige **that** well. What's going on?*

"I was talking to a colleague of mine here... she runs a small garden out in East County... and we were discussing the usual. Problems with boards. We thought it might be good to get together with another director or two to talk on an informal basis. Then we came up with the idea to have a small meeting with directors each bringing a board member. I'd really like you to come. All you'd need to do is buy a plane ticket. I could put you up here at the house... you might remember me telling you that La Jolla Gardens was once quite a luxurious residence... and almost all of your meals would be covered. It would be Friday evening through Sunday evening."

"That's quite an invitation. But pretty short notice..."

"I so hope you can come. I'd like to have somebody

who's been in the business a while and whose opinion I trust. There are... issues." Her voice dropped an octave on that last word.

"Well, I hope a little gathering of directors could help solve them. I'm going to have to get back to you."

"You have kids, I know. I'm just a bit... flummoxed, I guess you'd say."

That weekend is near the end of my parents' annual trip here. They could babysit. Frank will be out of town then, at that long-weekend park service training. It's hard to pass up a free stay in La Jolla. I'm pretty sure it's one of the wealthiest communities in the country. Not a place I'd normally be able to afford. A great place to decompress after the spring season here. And I can get a cheap ticket...

"How many directors do you want to host?"

"We could add another director/board member pair. Do you have anybody in mind?"

"Well, a friend of mine, Lila Busby, just became director of a garden in Copperton, New Mexico. It's a situation like yours, where the founder donated an estate to a nonprofit. The same way this garden started. Lila could probably use some moral support, too."

"It's lonely, isn't it. Being an executive director." She sounded wistful. Lonesome for a life before all the responsibility? Bea remembered Paige as an almost relentlessly upbeat, highly social person.

"Yeah, Paige, as a director, you're neither board nor staff. It's good to have peers."

"Exactly. I'd like to carve out some time for a heart-to-heart. A nice long beach walk."

"I'll get back to you. And if I decide to come, is it okay with you to see if Lila can make it?'

"Sure. I want it to be a small, intimate group. If you think she'll fit in, I trust you."

"Thanks. Send me an email with exact times and dates, okay?" She gave Paige her email address and ended the call.

That was a surprising conversation. Bea stared out her window at a cactus wren feeding her young in a cholla outside the office window. She thought about the little she knew about Paige Pearson. They'd taken some biology classes together, and Paige had been active in a student environmental group protesting the disastrous Exxon Valdez oil spill in Alaska. But after a summer back home in La Jolla, she'd started dating an MBA candidate, Monroe Something from the University of Southern California. She'd dropped out of their student organization, and by Christmas of their sophomore year, she'd dropped out of UC Santa Cruz and transferred to her boyfriend's school.

Bea had met the guy once. He was handsome, fit, well-coiffed, and dressed in name-brand outdoor gear. People probably would entrust their money to him, which is where his career path was going at the time.

He and Paige had gone out with Bea and a few others at a little Italian place that made great pesto, which Paige had loved in the early days. She'd started to order the pesto when he took charge. He insisted on veal saltimbocca for them both… so much for Paige's earlier vegetarian inclinations. He'd ordered pricey French wine instead of the cheap chianti they all favored and had poured it just for himself and Paige. Paige had seemed slightly embarrassed by his proprietary behavior, but she'd never let up on her light banter all evening.

Bea and Paige had lost touch with each other entirely after Paige left northern California, until they'd met again at the recent botanical garden annual conference. Paige had updated Bea then on her life in the intervening years. She and Monroe had moved to La Jolla where he'd gotten a job with an investment firm, and she'd gone to work in her father's hotel business. The marriage hadn't lasted.

Well, neither did my first marriage. You don't always make the wisest decisions in your early twenties. Bea thought fleetingly of Pat Flynn, her first husband. Childless life had been fun with him, full of concerts and dancing and spontaneous trips to the Sierras or New Orleans, but he surely wasn't cut out for the rigors of colic, diapers, preschool communicable diseases, and above all, 24/7 care.

Bea had told Paige she'd jumped at the chance to work in a botanical garden instead of a public school. Paige had said she'd been "over the moon" at the opportunity to apply for the job at La Jolla Gardens. "I wanted to get back to caring about the natural world. I think back on our days at UC Santa Cruz fondly," she'd said, over a glass of cabernet at the conference hotel bar. "All those hikes in the redwoods. Volunteering on Earth Day." She'd held Bea's eyes as she said this.

"Yeah, I wanted to find an earlier self after my own divorce. My ex called it my 'whole wheat and bare feet' persona."

Why not spend the weekend in La Jolla? She could take in deep, long lungfuls of sea air. Walk barefoot in the sand and get her feet wet, no matter how cold the Pacific was in April. Find sand dollars. And maybe make herself useful to other fellow directors, too.

Time to stop daydreaming about breaking waves. Time to face an early morning meeting with Angus.

She loved Angus. He'd been a kind of grandfather to her kids, which had been a godsend in her single-parent years. He was a dear, and a fine gardener, besides. But he was *not* happy with the Events Center, built a couple of years ago, nor what it had spawned. Angus called it "Weddings R Us." Her predecessor Ethan Prestons's plan to fix the garden's financial instability had been to build this center to attract rentals... especially weddings. He'd left the Gardens before the center was built, becoming a therapist instead of a boss and a fund raiser, but his plan was working. Except that all the crowds generated more work for the tiny gardening staff.

Angus began before he sat down. "Bea, we had to climb the cork oak to pull a slew of condoms out this morning. The thing looked like a damned Christmas tree. Every color in the rainbow, slid onto the leaves. Can I get hazard pay?"

She decided to take him head on. "You know we all got pay raises because of the income from the Events Center."

"Yes, I do know that, and I'm grateful, but we really need to think about more gardening staff. What with pulling condoms out of trees, and other assorted entertainment gambits from the gamboling hordes, things may not get planted or watered or pruned or weeded."

"It's a fair point. You guys do a lot, even without removing tree decorations. I'm working on it. I'm working on getting the money together for another gardener on staff."

"Thanks."

"Now my concern."

"No doubt it's Francie."

"I get it that she loves this place and wants to protect it. But shouting an obscenity at somebody who picked wildflowers in the back forty is not the way to handle it. I'll send you the URL for a paper that says that the number one complaint people have about cultural institutions is rude staff. Give it to Francie. And put a letter in her file."

"Yeah, I know I have to talk with her and write her up. The old days weren't so bad. The peace and quiet..."

"And practically no visitors. We're supposed to be a *public* garden."

Angus groaned and saluted.

That went better than I expected. Bea spent the rest of the day coordinating the details of the next weekend special event—a tour of home gardens throughout the city. One of the homeowners had gotten cold feet about having the public in her home, and all the publicity about it had already gone out. Bea calmed her down, and then went over the financials for the final spring event, the plant sale, with the bookkeeper. Their net was slightly under budget. By 5:00, she was quite ready to contemplate a relaxing weekend by the sea.

CHAPTER TWO

FRANK AND BEA WERE EXHALING after getting the kids in bed. Frank combed his fingers through Bea's short blonde bob. "You've got to stop putting in these hours. A break in La Jolla sounds like just the thing."

Bea reciprocated, running her fingers through his thick black curls. Her fingers got stuck, and she left them there and looked into his black eyes. "I'd rather spend time at the ocean with you. But since you'll be gone..."

"...and your parents will be here..."

"I'll go."

They headed to the bedroom without another word.

She called Lila, feeling quite relaxed, about an hour later. Lila, like Paige, wasn't an intimate friend. But Bea thought that she and Lila could be close; they simply hadn't spent much time together. Three years earlier, they'd bonded over the trials of single parenthood, although Lila's kids were now adults. Lila was a sculptor, and a former real estate agent. Bea would never have predicted that she'd become a botanical garden director.

Lila was all in. They'd chatted a bit.

"Okay, Bea, I can get behind going to La Jolla. I'm always up for a dose of ocean. And it would be fun to do this with you. And I'm likely to learn something, since I have no idea what I'm doing."

"I doubt that. But remind me how this came about. I know you told me, but... the motivation was that your old friend Gert MacKenzie wanted to go on the road and camp and not take care of the property anymore?"

"Yup."

"And so she donated the place to be a public garden. But I never got clear how you got inveigled into leaving your sculpting work to take the *very* left-brain job of executive director."

"Gert wouldn't take no for an answer. And there are only two other people on the board, and they're scared of Gert."

"Not surprising," Bea said with a laugh. "When I met her, she opened the door brandishing a broom. I got the impression she reveled in the witchy image."

"I'm quite sure she does. So, my other two board members do whatever Gert wants. I don't know, I thought it might be interesting to try this director job for a time, and you can be my mentor. And maybe these California folks can help me, who knows."

"I'm hardly an authority."

"Right now, I must say it's a whole lot of work."

"Yep. That won't change. Would you bring Gert with you?"

"Who else? I'm guessing she'll camp on the way out there and come stomping into the fancy La Jolla house smelling like a campfire and wearing cut-offs. It might be good for folks there."

"Or not."

"You know, it's kind of an interesting idea, having a director and one board member per garden to discuss a pressing issue at their respective institutions."

"Lila, I have a feeling our hostess wants some moral support for a particular issue. I guess we'll see."

"Enough about meetings. Catch me up on the important stuff. How are you liking being the big cheese? And I'm not clear on how exactly that happened for you, either. What became of the guy who was the director before you? The last time I saw you he was back in his job. And you and Frank finally got married?"

Bea sighed. "Okay. Let me get a glass of wine and I'll

catch you up." She came back to the phone in her slippers, with a glass of cabernet. She took a sip, closed her eyes, and began. "Well, you did know my old boss, Ethan, was in a coma because he was in a bike accident."

"That wasn't an accident. Some nut job tried to run him over, as I remember. But he recovered well enough was able to come back to his job. I guess I lost track of what happened after that."

"He did come back, but he had an epiphany during the long days of recovery. He realized what he really wanted to do was be a horticultural therapist. You know, helping people heal by caring for plants. Ethan credited his huge progress at the rehab center to the plants that friends gave him. He wanted to get certification as a horticultural therapist and work with people with mental health issues. He came back long enough for the board to conduct a search."

"And they picked you."

"They did. Maybe because it was the path of least resistance, since I had been the acting director while Ethan was out on medical leave."

"You undersell yourself."

"Maybe. I didn't apply right away, because I already knew there was a lot more stress involved than what I could go back to—volunteer coordinator/education director—and you know, the single parent thing."

"Yeah, it had to be hard for you to say, 'No, Mr. Donor, I can't meet you for breakfast, I don't have childcare at 7 a.m.'"

"Exactly. Plus the Frank issue."

"Frank became an issue."

"No. Well, yes. Well, he wasn't about to leave D.C., and although he briefly had Land Conservancy business in Arizona, he didn't anymore. And his mother had a caretaker, but he was her only family, and her emotional support, and she got worse. Her ALS was progressing super-fast. Frank needed to be around, and I couldn't go jetting off to the East Coast all the time, especially if I became director, with all those added responsibilities. But I took the job when it was offered to me. Frank and I agreed that we cared for one another. We never used the love word, not then. We decided we should be free to see other people. And we both did."

"I heard that sigh. So then what happened?"

Bea explained that they hadn't really clicked with the people they'd dated. It was a failed experiment. "I kept thinking about what Frank would have said or done. One clear night, I suggested that we go out and look at the Milky Way, and the guy I was dating wasn't interested in making a five-minute effort. And Frank said his girlfriend just gave him a puzzled look when he made 'attempted witticisms.' Plus, Frank wasn't so hot on living in DC and wearing a tie to work every day and dealing with the traffic. Plus..." There was a silence, which Lila broke.

"Plus, his mother died, I'm guessing."

"Yeah. I felt horrible to be so relieved about a death. But we both were, really. He hated watching her regress. Anyway, he applied for a job here and got it, with the park service. And we got back together, and he moved in, and we got married a year ago, in the Gardens."

"Are you living happily ever after?"

"He thinks I work too much. But he's great with the kids, and they enjoy him, and yes, we're doing well."

"Have you decided this executive director business is worth the hassles for you?"

"For now. How about you? Is your new garden worth the stress of starting up a big new project?"

"I haven't been doing it long enough to say. I'll let you know in a few months. It does keep me on my toes."

"Yup." Bea yawned, and said she had to go to bed.

"Go, go. We'll have fun together in this mansion, and Gert will liven things up."

"Your first idea sounds great. The second, unnerving."

Bea's parents had arrived in Tucson for their annual visit a few days after Paige's phone invitation; they'd all have more than a week together before Bea and Frank left on their respective trips. Bea's mother Emma was up early every morning. And perky about it. Even at sixty-five, she was as petite and trim as her daughter. And more organized, Bea reflected, as Emma laid out the activities she'd planned for the kids while Bea and Frank were both out of town. The first morning, Bea accepted a cup of espresso from her mother, which she'd prepared before Bea could get to the regular coffee pot.

"Yes, Mom, they love miniature golf, and you can never miss with the Desert Museum. Is Dad going along on all these field trips?"

"I certainly hope so. If it were up to him, you know, he'd be working on some paper for one of his butterfly journals, but I reminded him that he's retired now, and he doesn't get to see his grandkids very often!"

"Yesterday he told me he was thinking of abandoning his hearing aids because he had no idea his grandkids were so noisy."

"Yes, well..." Emma couldn't finish this sentence because Andy and his little sister Jessie emerged at the same time, arguing about which one of them owned the University of Arizona Wildcats tee shirt, because "it's way too small for you now, Andy," according to seven-year-old Jessie. "You already had it for *three years.* You got it when *you* were seven, Andy!" And after that everything was a whirl of find your backpack/ pack your lunch/ no, I did *not* buy Cheetos for your lunches/ that sweater has a rip in it/ finish your cereal/ you'll be late for the bus/ I'll be back Sunday night/ be good to your grandparents. I love you all.

Emma took the kids to the bus stop, and Bea's father Stanley emerged from the bedroom at this opportune time, his glasses at a precarious angle, his whitening hair arrayed in various tufts. He was looking quite a bit thinner than when she'd last seen him, when she and Frank and the kids had gone to visit her parents in central California last Christmas. The blue-black bags under his eyes were more noticeable than those kind hazel eyes behind the glasses.

"Sleep ok, Dad?"

"Sure honey. Don't worry. We'll all be fine here when you go to the beach. Is that what's worrying you? And we'll all be together for a good while before that. You always were a worrier."

She gave her father a hug. He was bony as could be.

Her dad spent the next week or so giving the kids a tutorial on butterflies. He'd brought them each a net. He took them out to urban arroyos after school, and they caught tons of the lovely creatures, setting them free after they'd all identified each butterfly with field guide pictures. The kids were psyched about the weekend field trips he would take them on while their parents were gone... mini golf took a back seat on their wish list. In the evenings, her mother joined them in making a butterfly collage from pictures in magazines. Bea and Frank went to work every day without having to worry about after-school pick-up arrangements, and they managed to go out to dinner twice without kids, an unheard-of and deeply appreciated luxury.

The day before Bea left, Frank headed to northern California for his park service training. He'd be in the wilds of northern California, she'd be on the southern California coast, and her kids would be tramping around the Sonoran Desert with her parents. A perfect weekend for all. Nothing could chip Bea's smooth contentment.

There weren't even any work crises. Bea stared out

her office window at the shadows the mesquite leaves made on the brick walkways. She had to finish one grant proposal, start another, and gently point out the infeasibility of a certain donor's fundraising idea... to create a holiday event called "White Christmas in the Desert" with real snow. All over the whole garden. Should she emphasize the water conservation in the desert issue? Maybe just check out the cost of snow-making machines. That ought to do it.

Paige called in the middle of all this.

"Bea, it'll be just six of us. The East County director I invited had something come up at her garden, and she can't afford to take the weekend off."

"Too bad! We could have offered her some director-solidarity."

"Yeah, well. Something's come up here, too."

"You mentioned that."

"No, something new. Something I absolutely need time alone with you to discuss."

"Of course, Paige."

"Remind me again of some good reasons to be a non-profit director."

"Well, it feels great when you can accomplish some good things for the garden, for your community, and even, in your tiny way, for the environment. But..."

"But what?"

"But it's a lot of responsibility for not very much pay. And you have to figure out how to dance with a bunch of board members who are all your bosses, but whose garden job is a small voluntary commitment."

"Yup. That's the part I'm... struggling with." The last two words were lost in a sniffle.

"We'll hash things out, Paige."

"Thanks, Bea. See you soon." Her voice was stronger now. It was the voice of the self-assured socialite Bea knew.

After she hung up, Bea found herself staring at the birds outside her window. *I really hope I can help her out. Meanwhile, I have to make sure Angus is on top of things here while I'm gone.*

Their meeting went fine. Then Angus asked, "Are your parents going to be able to keep up with your kids this weekend? Your dad has aged since I last saw him."

"He's ten years older than my mom. Getting a little frail, yeah. But she can handle them. She was a fourth-grade schoolteacher!"

"Ten-four, boss. Have fun at the beach. Don't eat too many bonbons out on that beach towel!"

"I suspect that'll be the least of my worries."

CHAPTER THREE

As she was driving Frank's beat-up Nissan to long term airport parking—she had left the SUV for her parents—she thought about the group she would be spending the weekend with. There was Paige, who was having trouble adjusting to her job. She'd come straight from the hotel industry. People often thought that business leadership translated directly to nonprofit leadership. But they sometimes didn't realize that businesses are about profit, and nonprofits have to stay solvent, of course, but they are about fulfilling their missions. Bea remembered a gardener who'd said to her, "This is the first job I've ever had where the bosses know less than anybody lower down." The gardener had been privy to another "White Christmas in the Desert"-type idea, another doozy that Bea'd had to quash. A board member had been inspired to propose a bike race through the grounds. "What about my plants?" the gardener had cried, in anguish. No doubt Paige had a similar story to report.

Bea didn't know who Paige's board member would be.

Bea was bringing Margaret Rhodes. They didn't know each other well, but Margaret had supported Bea back when she'd been struggling as acting director because her boss Ethan had been out on medical leave. Bea had been thinking of asking her board president, Alicia Vargas, but Alicia had mentioned that Margaret might want to go, since she had been summering in La Jolla for years.

It turned out that Margaret's house was not far from La Jolla Gardens. "The couple who used to live at what's now the botanical gardens were dear friends. I'd love to see what's happening on the property. And how Paige is managing."

Was there a dip of condescension in her tone when she mentioned Paige's name?

And now there would be just four others in their little gathering, since the East County duo had dropped out. Bea would catch up with Lila on the plane. And then there was the inimitable Gert MacKenzie. Bea wondered if she'd had any more run-ins with the law. The last time she'd seen her, Gert and her husband had nearly been arrested for conspiring to steal ancient Native American pottery from public lands. Gert hadn't been charged then, but Bea had thought that the MacKenzies' role hadn't been quite up to the smell test.

Even if the meetings got strange or tedious or weren't particularly helpful, Bea and Lila could go for beach walks.

The woman in the Southwest Airlines check-in line wearing a bright yellow turtleneck, a long paisley skirt and boots was, of course, Lila Busby of Copperton, New Mexico. Bea recognized the long curly silver tresses even before Lila turned to greet her. They compared boarding passes as they headed to the blessedly short security line. Bea had gotten her boarding pass the moment Southwest allowed her to; exactly twenty-four hours before flight time. She was in the "A" boarding group. Lila was in the last "C" group, because she hadn't known to jump on the boarding pass business.

"Obviously, I need to get out more. I didn't know you had to jump on your boarding pass so ridiculously fast," Lila said with a shrug, as the two friends sat down to put their shoes back on after the indignities of the security check.

"Yeah, that's the way Southwest does it, Lila. But I can

save you a seat."

Bea turned to greet Margaret Rhodes, who was replacing black flats with gold buckles. After Lila zipped up her boots, she lent Margaret a hand to stand. She tottered a little. How old was Margaret? Bea wasn't sure. Older than her mother. Quite a bit older than her mother.

Bea looked at the two of them. Margaret's face pinched inward; Lila had wide-set gray eyes and high, spreading cheeks. Margaret wore her trademark skirt and pearls and carried a Louis Vuitton handbag, and had short, wavy white, sprayed-down hair. Lila's silver tresses had escaped both barrettes.

"Thank you, Lila, you're a dear. You two sit together. I've just got to finish my murder mystery, so I won't be much company on the plane."

"I plan to ask Bea lots of questions, Margaret, so Bea and I *have* to sit together."

Bea groaned.

As Bea made her halting way with the "A numbers 31-60" crowd, stopping every few seconds for those who had to hoist bulging bags into the overhead, she passed Margaret, who had pre-board status. She was already engrossed in a paperback with a glittering bloody knife on the cover. Bea found aisle and middle seats for herself and Lila, who arrived with the very last boarding group, "C numbers 31-60." Lila looked to be number C 59; she really *had* been late to get her boarding pass.

Lila stowed her roller bag, buckled her seat belt, put a zip-up purse with yellow-and red-Indian elephants under the seat in front of her, and began, "This Paige person, our hostess in California? She's an old college buddy of yours? That's why you were invited to this thing, and why you were able to shoehorn me in?"

Bea had forgotten how those gray eyes could focus on you. Lila was a listener. The rare kind: the kind who was genuinely interested in what you had to say.

"No! Not a buddy. But part of my gang my freshman year at UC Santa Cruz. Then she transferred to the University of Southern California, which probably was a way better fit for her."

"You're going to have to say more than that, Bea." Lila's whole face creased into a smile. She'd spent years in the sun at high elevation, bringing on prolific wrinkles, but the smile lines around her eyes and mouth charmed Bea. She thought, as she had earlier, that she'd be lucky to look like Lila in her mid-fifties.

"Well, USC is generally more conservative than Santa Cruz. When Paige was at Santa Cruz, she went from joining protest marches to telling us we were 'naïve about the cost of doing business.' Now I guess she has ping-ponged back a bit. This garden is in the neighborhood she grew up in. The property belonged to family friends whom she'd known her whole life. Maybe being there gave her a way to integrate her roots with her environmental leanings. I don't know. I'm just speculating. She lives in a mansion on site; it's one of the perks of the job. Just like ours, huh."

Lila chuckled. "A little hard to imagine, I agree. Well, we get to stay in the house for the weekend. A good enough perk."

"Yeah. It'll be amazing to see. There's a world-class cycad collection and a tropical aviary."

They ordered sparkling waters from the flight attendant, stocked up on peanuts, and Bea continued.

"Paige said there are eight bedrooms in this mansion, so there's room for all of us. She said most of us even have our own bathrooms."

"Sounds like overkill, but I'm not complaining," Lila said. "Unless my carefully wrapped three ounces of prickly pear syrup breaks open in my suitcase."

"I thought it was cool to ask us to bring something made from plants of our regions. My mesquite loaf should travel pretty well. But tell me about Eddy."

Eddy had a band that played "Americana and folk," and Lila said were getting bookings throughout the Southwest.

"I'm getting tired of all his traveling, but he loves it. Success at 55," Lila said.

It was a short flight, and before long, the plane began to descend into a cloud bank. When it emerged, they were a few hundred feet above downtown buildings of San Diego. Bea gulped. She looked around at the other passengers. No one seemed fazed by their near collision with skyscrapers. *Okay, so this is normal.* The airport must be in the middle of the city, which was very dense and hilly. *People who live and work in this part of town must be half-deaf from the noise.*

Then she caught sight of the blue ocean, stretching forever to the west.

Lila, in the aisle seat, stood up quickly when the seat belt sign went off. A few minutes later, she sighed. "I always forget how long it takes to actually get out the door."

"Everyone does," Bea said. "Hope springs eternal."

They walked into a terminal swarming with people. Every seat was filled; people were lined up to board in several snaking lines. A child was screaming to the left, and two toddlers were trying to escape over on the right, pursued by a mother who might regret, at some later date, their hearing her epithets. The whole place smelled like a taco franchise, as opposed to one of Tucson's great Mexican restaurants. Grease, hamburger, a hint of salsa that was more closely related to ketchup than pico de gallo.

A man with a briefcase came towards them at a run, clipping Bea's arm with the heavy case. "Ow!" she said, but he just gave her a curt nod and sped up.

As they followed the crowd to the escalators, Bea grimaced and said to Lila, "We're going to have to recalibrate." Each step on the escalator contained a human being. Such was the difference between a metro area of fewer than a million and one three times that big.

"Honey, I'm the one from a town with 10,000 people. Imagine how I feel."

Bea and Lila walked out into the cool air.

"My god, it's so humid!" Lila said, just as Bea exclaimed, "Oh, I've missed that smell!" It brought back her college days in Santa Cruz, and she had a brief memory of a sunset walk on the beach with a boy she hadn't thought about for years.

They hailed a cab to La Jolla Gardens. Margaret had told Bea she'd catch her own cab to her La Jolla vacation home. "Tell dear Paige I'll be along shortly." As Margaret got into her cab, Bea thought about the fact that Margaret's La Jolla buddies had endowed their property with ten million dollars. Bea reflected, not for the first time, that it would be lovely if Margaret was inspired by their example.

In the cab, Bea put on her sweater... it was about twenty-five degrees cooler than the mid-eighty-degree desert sunshine she'd left in Tucson, and it was so very cloudy. The freeway was slightly terrifying; Bea remembered that the key in California was to drive fast, change lanes fast, and never to hesitate. Good thing she didn't have to drive here. When they exited the freeway, there was a car stopped at the yield sign, clearly as flummoxed by the traffic tearing by on the surface street as Bea herself was.

"Zonies," muttered the driver.

"Zonies?" Lila asked.

"Damned Arizonans. They come flooding out of Phoenix and Tucson, and they don't know how to drive. Or swim."

"I'm from Arizona," Bea said, trying to keep her tone mild.

"Beg your pardon, ma'am." He didn't say it in a begging tone.

The traffic on the surface street continued to be only slightly less alarming, than the freeway rush. They passed some sterile-looking university buildings and were quite suddenly on a street lined with huge homes, most of them behind walls, hedges, or elaborately designed fencing Bea opened her window and caught her first bracing whiff of salt air and wet kelp.

"The houses on the left overlook the ocean, up on top of the cliff there, said the cab driver. "La Jolla is the most expensive part of the City of San Diego, and it is definitely San Diego—has the same utilities and everything—but it has that magic zip code."

"My Lord, there's a lot of grass," Lila said.

"And a lot of gardeners," Bea observed. The street was full of guys packing up their beat-up pickup trucks for the day. Shovels, chainsaws, leaf blowers and lawnmowers were being hoisted into truck beds. A couple of workers were just finishing a pink-and-white petunia-filled border as a BMW pulled up and a gentleman in a three-piece suit emerged, giving the gardeners a quick nod. Bea turned around to watch him collect his mail and disappear behind a boxwood hedge obscuring the house.

"Gardeners aren't the only ones who don't live here," Lila said. Bea's head swiveled forward to see a very muscular young man dressed only in a towel with a rolled-down wetsuit underneath it. He leaned over to remove the bottom of the wetsuit as they drove by. The towel stayed in place.

"Yeah, there's a road the surfers walk to get down to the beach near here," the cab driver volunteered.

They rounded a corner and saw bumper-to-bumper vans and small sedans, all with roof racks, many of them surrounded by people in various stages of undress, surrounded by surfboards. One of them was pouring a gallon of water on his head.

"Guess the area isn't totally exclusive," Bea said.

The cab driver turned around and said, "I wouldn't say that," just as a small private security car cruised by. "We're here, ladies," he announced pulling into a long driveway marked by a wooden sign proclaiming "La Jolla Gardens" in elegant cursive.

"Quite a driveway," Lila remarked without expression. A ten-or-twelve-foot-high marble fountain with carved lions sat in the center of the semicircular drive.

"Indeed," was about all Bea could manage before the cab parked in front of a huge brick home. "This belongs in Virginia. On a plantation."

Lila chuckled. "Yes, it's called Georgian architecture. After several King Georges of England in the 18th and 19th century."

Bea turned around to look at Lila after this pronouncement. "Remember, Bea, I was in real estate for a time in New Mexico. Where there aren't a lot of Georgian mansions. But you also know that I'm originally from Pennsylvania. My father was, in fact, a big deal real estate guy there. Pennsylvania has its share of exclusive neighborhoods, of course." Lila looked like she wanted to say something else, but a figure emerged from the columns framing the doorway of the house shouting

"Welcome!"

Bea emerged from the cab to hug Paige, who was tall, svelte, and blonde. Bea's equally blonde head reached just below the woman's chin.

Lila was paying the driver, and as he drove off, the woman came over to Lila. "Hello! I'm Paige."

Lila stepped forward, her hand outstretched. "Lila Busby." Paige blinked her eyes once in surprise as they shook, no doubt taken aback by the roughness of Lila's gardener-and-sculptor hands. Bea took a closer look at her college acquaintance. She was older, of course; they'd graduated more than twenty years before, and Bea still held the image of that young woman in her mind, despite having seen her more recently. But Paige's eyes were awfully puffy, and she seemed to have a bit of a tremor in her hand.

Her words felt genuinely welcoming. "I'm *so* glad you could come. Come in and let's get you both settled."

Paige led them into the foyer. There was an ornate chandelier that would have fit at Versailles, but the paintings were of a different era entirely... eight huge pastel semi-abstract botanicals lined the walls. Paige explained their sleeping arrangements. "We have a wealth of bedrooms here, so everybody who's staying the night gets their own. I'm over in the south wing, with both of you and Gert Mackenzie. Tonight's speaker is staying over in the north wing. He'll leave tomorrow after breakfast, but he seemed interested in spending the night. My board member Hank Archer lives locally and he's bringing an incoming board member who lives in the neighborhood. So *they* won't be staying the night!" She laughed, and Bea detected a false note. "Oh, and there's Camila Gomez who's helping out with meals this weekend. She used to work for my family, but she lives so far from La Jolla... she's in a bedroom close to the kitchen." Bea and Lila exchanged a look that Paige didn't seem to notice as she went on. "Margaret Rhodes will be at her own place, as you know."

"Margaret tells me she's an old family friend?" Bea asked.

"She and my parents go way back. She has summered in this neighborhood forever." Paige neutral tone and flat expression could mean most anything. She continued with more animation, "Of course everybody will be here for dinner. That is, if Gert gets into town from her desert camping trip, Lila! She left a message that she was having too much fun to hurry here." Again, there was a forced laugh. "So I'll show you all to your rooms and we can meet in an hour for a glass of wine before dinner, right here," she said, showing them a huge living room filled with white furniture. The traditional architecture did not extend to the windows. *Why would it,* Bea thought. *Anyone with the money to do it would have these huge picture windows facing the Pacific Ocean. Facing west, no less... perfect for sunsets.*

"I hope I can find my way back here," Lila said dryly.

Paige smiled graciously. "I'm sure you will. And by the way, here's the front door key for each of you. But I doubt you'll need it. We keep things open during the day, but in case you have a night on the town... The security guard arms the door when everyone's turned in for the night and disarms it before he goes off shift at 7 in the morning."

Bea discovered that her room featured not only her own bathroom, but a bathtub jacuzzi, as well. From the second floor, the view of the waves rolling in up the coast made the whole trip worthwhile. But they were far below her. The houses in this neighborhood were hundreds of feet above the beach.

Bea opened the French doors onto a balcony and stared at the water for a while. The waves were dotted with surfers. She couldn't see the beach right below the Gardens because of the steep drop-off. A large green lawn crept right up to the edge, and sprawling lawn chairs were arranged around a fire pit, near a fishpond. And if it was shade you wanted, there was a white gazebo with a couch swing facing the ocean, several wicker chairs with fluffy cushions, and a telescope, no less. A big one. It would probably be too cloudy to see stars that night, but maybe a whale during the daytime? There seemed to be some flagging tape beyond the gazebo, and Bea figured the garden had to keep visitors away from the cliff edge, for liability reasons. She looked around for the "specialty gardens" that she'd seen in the brochure Paige had sent with her invitation, and noticed a large, raised vegetable bed. Andy would like the cycads surrounding it—he knew they were around at the time of his beloved dinosaurs. He even drew them into his dinosaur pictures; his cycads looked like short palm trees, which was sort of accurate. Bea wished her family could see this place.

There were agaves around the vegetable beds, too—maybe the coastal variety that Bea knew to be native. A couple of them were shooting up beautiful yellow flowering stalks. Bea squinted at what looked like the pink bracts of South African king protea flowers. She hoped they'd have time to see the gardens before dinner; she really wanted a closer look at all these plants.

Something in the sky caught her eye. My God, it was a hang glider. Coming from the right, no doubt off the huge high cliffs north of them. The cliffs must be providing updrafts. Well, if people fell, they'd go into the water. The ocean seemed a safer landing spot than the land. At least she hoped so. She noticed that some had only one pilot, and some had two. Maybe one was an instructor? She caught her breath as two gliders almost collided. Maybe they had it all under control; she certainly didn't know. They were brightly colored and graceful in gray skies, and she settled into watching them dance.

Lila emerged on the adjacent balcony and waved. When she showed up, Gert would probably be in a room on the other side of her, with a similarly-sized balcony. Way down on the end was the premiere balcony, the royal box in this opera of a house. There were reasons to be jealous of Paige's perks, but quite honestly, Bea would rather be a visitor here.

She watched the hang gliders for a few more minutes, and then went inside, feeling a little chilled. She showered, and checked email... *oh good, no pre-weekend crises at Shandley Gardens, or with the kids.* She called home and found the whole family was jazzed about having seen two coyotes on one of her father's favorite pastimes, a dusk drive in the desert. They were doing fine without her.

She took a look at herself in the overly large bathroom mirror before heading downstairs. *I really don't need that much detail.* She saw a fine-featured woman with close-cropped hair that gave her a bit of an elven look. She reapplied her lip gloss. *That's going to have to do. How in the world can I be the most experienced executive director at this little gathering?* She raised an eyebrow at the young woman in the mirror.

She found her way down the marble staircase to the living room, where Paige was sipping wine. Bea had just raised a glass of pinot grigio to her lips when the front door burst open. Bea nearly spilled the whole glass of wine on her dress and Paige jumped up, wincing as Gert Mackenzie, Lila's board member, stomped in wearing heavy hiking boots, jeans, and the distinct aroma of a sweaty desert hike.

"Pretty fancy place you got here," she said. "Hello, Bea, I know you're not in charge. Who is?"

"Hello, Mrs. Mackenzie."

"Gert's the name!" she remonstrated.

"I'm Paige Pearson, the executive director here." Paige held out her hand. She wiped it discreetly on her slacks after a handshake. "Let me show you your room and you can freshen up before the others get here." Before she could lead Gert away, the doorbell rang. "If you'll excuse me for just a minute, I'll let this person in and then I can take you up."

"No hurry," said Gert. "I'm pretty hungry. Hope dinner's soon. I can go upstairs later."

Bea pointed out the spread of soft cheeses and fine crackers, and poured Gert a glass of red. "If you're gonna drink wine, it oughtta be red," was Gert's answer when Bea asked what wine she'd like.

Paige emerged with a well-put-together man about Lila's age wearing a polo shirt, khakis, Top-siders, and a brilliant smile.

"Hello, ladies, I'm Hank Archer, President of the Board of La Jolla Gardens. With whom do I have the pleasure of dining this evening?"

They introduced themselves. Bea tried to summon her most gracious persona as she smiled and shook hands. Gert didn't offer her hand, but did volunteer her name, in her usual piercing tone. Bea was impressed that Hank's gaze didn't falter as he took in Gert's cocktail garb.

Bea took a closer look at Hank. He seemed familiar, somehow. He was the kind of guy who had always been handsome, and who'd always known he was handsome. Many women had no doubt reinforced this certainty. A little gray hair probably made him even more appealing to younger women. *Frank's good-looking, too, but he doesn't radiate that knowledge. I wonder what he'd make of this crew.* She stifled a laugh, and Hank turned his head with an enquiring look.

Bea realized that he reminded her a great deal of an older version of Paige's old boyfriend Monroe.

Lila emerged from her room above them and came down the long winding staircase. "Another lovely lady," Hank said, with that dazzling smile.

How could teeth be that white? Well, they couldn't of course, without some dental help. Maybe you had to look perfect here, since you could afford to. What a burden that would be! She thought briefly about her dear father with his wispy hair and holey old shirts. He didn't even think women should wear makeup. He'd appreciate Gert.

Lila had changed into a long, loose indigo-colored dress, with brightly colored combs in her long, wavy gray hair. She'd traded her boots for some painted clogs. She didn't look too startled at Gert's outfit at this toney event, either, and she shot Bea a quick *what-can-you-do* look when Paige again offered to take her to her room, and Gert again refused.

Hank shook Lila's hand and did not react to its roughness, as Paige had.

The doorbell rang again, and Margaret entered, trailed by a stooped, white-haired older man leaning heavily on a cane. Hank rushed to kiss Margaret's cheek. She gave him an affectionate pat on the shoulder. Paige walked up to her, and the two women engaged in a formal, utterly polite handshake. *It doesn't look like they're such close family friends. Maybe it's just Paige's parents who're close to Margaret.*

The other gentleman was smiling benignly at them.

Hank Archer introduced him with, "Max Danes has lived in this neighborhood forever. He'll be joining our board in July." Mr. Danes nodded to Paige. "Thank you so much for inviting someone who hasn't yet joined your esteemed board."

"Delighted to have you." Paige had clearly been well trained in the social graces. Who knew if she was unhappy that Hank Archer had brought a second board member... Bea's invitation had clearly stated that it was to be an intimate gathering with one board member plus the executive director.

Everyone settled into the billowy white cushions on the sofas and chairs.

Paige broke into their conversations. "So let me outline the weekend for you, and then we'll have a tour and go in to dinner. Thanks for bringing something that represents your garden to our potluck! I know it was a challenge for those of you who flew. This is the menu... see if I get it right. I've made halibut with lime from our garden, and nopalito salad. Bea made mesquite loaf cake for dessert, and Lila's made us some prickly pear syrup to top the cake with. Looks like the prickly pear is well represented, with salad from the pads and juice from the fruits!" They all nodded. "Hank, Max and Margaret got a pass on this," she said with a smile. "And of course there's more wine."

"Kind of you to give us a pass, Paige," Max Danes said, in his courtly manner.

"Of course," Paige said. Bea was thinking they would have had to ask their cooks to create something.

"And I've got some of my famous mesquite/prickly pear mead," Gert interjected. "For after dinner. If you're still standing."

Paige gave her a nod. "Thanks. Well, as you know, we're all bringing a problem to discuss that divides our boards. We'll mention those issues over dinner, and then we can discuss them in detail tomorrow."

"But first let's see the gardens!" Bea said.

"Of course! That's the first order of business. Also, we have a treat after dinner. A distinguished botanist, who will probably also join our board in July, will dine with us. Over coffee, he'll give us a little talk about water conservation."

Lila shot Bea a look. She already knew neither one of them saw this as La Jolla Gardens' strong suit, after one look at the ostentatious fountain. And the expansive grassy lawn and tropical vegetation.

"Yes, that will be interesting," Max Danes said, in a neutral tone. "Hank was kind enough to let me attend tonight's festivities because I'm so interested in his talk. But I'm afraid I must beg off on the walk." He gestured to his cane.

"The main pathways are Americans with Disabilities Act-accessible," Paige said.

"Thank you, my dear. You go on. I'm rather tired, and I have my paper." He unfurled *The Wall Street Journal.*

Bea reflected that she wouldn't want a new board member who would refuse this tour. But maybe she wasn't being fair. Maybe he was in pain. And he could probably help with funding and fund raising.

Paige seemed unfazed by his refusal, and continued, "Of course. We'll catch up with you at dinnertime. So… after we go over the issues tomorrow morning, everybody's free to take a beach walk, or go into town, or whatever. The Gardens is going to treat you all to a nice dinner in town tomorrow night. Then we wrap up Sunday morning. So freshen up your drinks, grab your jackets… I expect you desert folks will need them, with our humidity and ocean breezes. Let's go outside!"

CHAPTER FOUR

"YOU GOT YOURSELF QUITE A deal here, honey, livin' in a mansion with grounds like these!" Gert said aloud what most of them were probably thinking, as they walked out to as setting sun illuminating a few acres of lawn, punctuated by small garden areas. Seagulls swooped and called overhead.

Hank interjected quickly. "Paige grew up in this neighborhood. That's why the board thought she'd be such a natural for this job. Getting along with our neighbors is a top priority for us here. As you'll see when we get to our problem statements."

"Although there have always been plenty of disagreements in this little corner of the world," Margaret said, with what was supposed to be a laugh. Bea looked over at Hank, who'd cocked his head in surprise. Or was it mock surprise?

"Let's head towards the aviary," Paige said, cutting off any conversation about controversies.

They walked to the koi pond, which Paige said needed to be stocked constantly because of predatory birds. They saw the aviary, with its assortment of tropical birds. Bea felt discombobulated, watching bright toucans in the steamy jungle of a greenhouse, and emerging into graying skies and gray-green plants, cooled by a light sea breeze.

Paige led them to the cycads. She opened her mouth to say something, but Hank jumped in with, "This is the most valuable cycad collection in any small public garden. More valuable than those in much larger gardens, in fact.

Of course you all know that these are not dwarf palm trees, as some of our more ignorant visitors might suspect. They may have covered the earth at the time of the dinosaurs, but they're endangered now. Each one of our plants is worth tens of thousands to hundreds of thousands of dollars! We have species from Africa, Australia, Asia, and the Americas. That's why we need our own private security guards. They work from seven to seven every night. You'll meet Ace, who's on tonight."

"That's different from the guard we saw driving by in the car?" Lila asked.

Paige responded, "Yes, that guard is employed by the neighborhood."

They ranged through the collection of the odd-looking cycads, some of them a few feet high, and some several times that, but all with rough cylindrical trunks crowned by stiff dissected leaves. Huge gold cones grew in their centers.

"They could film Jurassic Park here," Gert said.

The only sound was the snapping of cameras, except when Hank pointed out the most valuable specimen, worth, he said, "about five hundred thousand dollars, but we don't tell our visitors that."

"Very impressive, Hank," Margaret said.

"The money or the plants?" Gert asked.

"Well, both, of course." Margaret looked to Bea for help, and Bea gave a neutral smile.

Paige moved them on. "So... you desert folks may be interested in our agave garden... we have eight species here, some of which you may recognize. We're pretty excited about these octopus agaves. The original owners planted them as pups ten years ago, and now look at this one in flower!! More little yellow flowers come out every morning, winding their way up the spike."

Bea studied the display. Shandley Gardens had two mature octopus agaves, and she'd always loved their three-foot swirly tentacle-like leaves. But she'd never seen one in flower, since it was a one-time occurrence before the plant up and died from the effort. Paige was right to exclaim at the one in bloom, its fifteen-foot spike covered with tiny golden flowers almost all the way to the top. Dozens of bees swirled around the spike, each landing on a different flower.

The other agave in flower was, indeed, the coast agave native to southern California, just as she'd thought while looking out her bedroom window. Its tough basal leaves were formidable; sharp and toothed, edged with red. The ten-foot flowering stalk branched out with yellow flowers with bits of red. A fuchsia-throated Anna's hummingbird whizzed around the flowers and bees, and then stuck its beak in a beeless flower to sip some nectar.

"I love this plant. I don't suppose it would grow in the Sonoran Desert," Bea said, as she took its picture. "But I suspect it likes its ocean breezes."

"Yes," Paige replied. "They're endangered plants and we're going to try to propagate lots of them."

"They may like the ocean breezes but they probably don't like the coastal development," Lila said. Hank gave her a sharp look.

Paige took them through the South Africa garden, which blew Bea's socks off with its king proteas. "Yes, our guests love these. This flower has a twelve-inch diameter!" Paige enthused.

Bea pulled out her phone to photograph these flowers, as did everyone else. Yellow and red tubular flowerets were cupped by stiff pink bracts. A king flower with a pink crown.

"I see why it's the national flower of South Africa," Lila said.

"Yes, the South African coast has a similar climate and soils," Paige responded.

Bea had a question. "These are all low-water-use

plants. But you have a huge lawn area. Have you gotten any negative feedback about that in a public garden in southern California?"

"You tell, her, honey!" Gert clapped Bea on the back. Bea fought her instinct to pull away.

"Well, uh... we are having discussions right now about returning much of the lawn area to coastal sage scrub."

"Some of us on the board think that's not the place of a botanical garden. There are plenty of those bushes in natural areas around here, including practically next door along the road to the sea. They aren't particularly spectacular." Hank definitely had an opinion about this.

He wasn't finished with this topic. "I mean, even the name. Coastal sage *scrub.*"

Bea said, "Well... I guess that depends upon what you see as the purpose of a public garden. There's always interest in gee-whiz stuff, but don't we have a responsibility to demonstrate environmental stewardship?"

Hank's face was beginning to flush red.

"It will be so great to hash these issues out with our peers this weekend!" Paige said. Bea began to understand why she'd wanted to convene this little meeting. Did she need moral support for her positions against her board president?

"The sun's about to set!" Bea said. She said she wanted to catch the "green flash," that moment the sun's light refracted into different colors, resulting in a moment of bright green on the horizon just as the sun sank.

"Too much marine layer for that tonight," Paige said. "That's those clouds on the horizon. But let's take a moment to watch the sunset. It's always worth it."

Bea reflected once again that she'd been a fool to harbor even a slight regret about leaving Tucson for a weekend of this. As they stood on the lawn, facing the sea, the sky went pink, and then orange. Bea's spirits rose with the colors, and then settled into peacefulness in the soft, sea-scented gathering twilight.

"We have just enough light left to see the vegetable garden," Paige announced, and hurried them towards a raised bed that stretched for a good twenty feet. Arugala, lettuce, kale, tomatoes, broccoli and cauliflowers ripened in neat rows. There was a patch of raspberries on one side of the vegetables, but they weren't ripe yet. The citrus were, though. They'd already gone by in Tucson. La Jolla Gardens had about six trees. The planters were partial to kumquats, it seemed, although there were also lemons and limes.

"Who eats all those fruits and vegetables?" Lila asked.

"Maybe you'll have to tear those out, too," Gert said.

"Well, we send almost all of our fruits and veggies to the food bank!" Paige gave her long hair a little toss.

"I'm curious... who ate them all before that?" Lila asked.

"Well, the family who lived here, I guess," Paige said.

"Musta had a whole heckuva lot of kids," Gert observed.

Bea noticed that Margaret started to say something but stopped herself.

"Lordy. Or a lot of parties! Well, let's eat!" Gert cut in.

"We have solar path lights all the way back to the house, fortunately," Paige said. They followed the lights in the gathering darkness.

A couple of bats swooped by. In the quiet, Bea was aware of the sound of the waves breaking below, and the soft breeze against her cheeks.

And they went into dinner, to discover that the "visiting botanist" who was giving the evening program was one of Bea's least favorite people on Earth. There he was, in his trademark Hawaiian shirt and flip flops. She was unsurprised to see him brazenly appraising his hostess's charms.

Paige ignored his look, and said, with grace, "This is

Dr. Armando Ramos, who'll be giving a fascinating talk after dinner."

Lila put her arm around Bea and whispered in her ear, "I remember you talking about this guy during that mess three years ago."

Paige looked at the huddling women with concern.

I hope Lila's whisper was quiet enough.

Paige said, "Dr. Ramos may be joining our board in July, like Mr. Danes."

Bea realized that Paige was not on a first-name basis with either of them, unlike Hank Archer. Although she'd noticed that Danes had called Paige by *her* first name earlier.

"Dr. Ramos will give us a little post-dinner presentation about water conservation," Paige explained.

"Bea, what an unexpected pleasure," Armando said with a leer. He was sporting a new brushy mustache that rendered him what Bea's mother would have called devilishly handsome.

"It's certainly unexpected," Bea responded. "Are you on the faculty somewhere in San Diego now?" He'd been denied tenure at the University of Arizona when he was on the Shandley Gardens' board.

"I do a little teaching, mostly consulting."

Bea nodded, but she was thinking that was an awfully vague answer.

Paige seemed to notice some tension, because she jumped in with a cheery, "I've put out place cards." When Gert snorted, Paige said, "Just so we can all get to know each other better."

"You got maids and everything like 'Downton Abbey'?" Gert asked.

"Oh, no, Camila is just helping us out for the weekend," Paige responded.

Hank gave Gert a cold, cold look.

Camila turned out to be a rather beautiful young

Latina in a uniform not quite out of a 19th century British mystery, but close enough. It was a long-sleeved black dress and black flats, covered by a white apron. Bea thanked her for her halibut; indeed, it looked delicious. Camila just nodded. Lila asked her in Spanish if she'd made the dish, and Camila said in English, and with no accent whatsoever, that no, Ms. Pearson had. Still no eye contact. Lila shot Bea another quick look. Armando thanked Camila for his plate, in Spanish, and gave her chest a quick once-over. *Some things will never change.*

The fish was flaky, succulent, and tangy with cumin and lime. The nopalitos weren't gummy, as they could sometimes be, and the salad included a bright and sumptuous mix of fresh tomatoes, cilantro, avocado, queso fresco and lime juice. There were lovely steaming-fresh corn tortillas on the side. Bea would rather have enjoyed every bite without having to hear about her colleagues' problems, but she was a guest here. Naturally, Gert did not hold back.

"This is damned good fish. I vote we finish it up before we hear about whatever's got your board's knickers in a knot," she proclaimed. And they complied with Gert's wishes.

Camila came out through the swinging doors between the dining room and kitchen and poured a delicious French chardonnay, and Bea noted that they were already on bottle number four when the mesquite pound cake with prickly pear sauce came around. But not everyone was drinking hard. Margaret had barely touched her wine, and Max was sipping slowly, but Armando, Hank, Gert and Paige were putting it away. Paige cleared her throat. "Okay, who wants to do their problem statement first?"

Bea looked around the table. Lila shook her head. Paige was smiling at Bea with what seemed to be an expectant look. "Okay," Bea said. "Margaret, jump in if I don't say this properly." Margaret nodded. Gert and Armando were pouring themselves generous glasses from the latest bottle that Camila had brought to the table. Armando was studying Paige. "Studying" was a kind term for it.

"Here's the thing," Bea began. "We all agree that we want as many locals as possible to enjoy and learn from Shandley Gardens. You pretty much have to own a car to get there; you *can* take public transportation, but it takes forever from downtown and you'd still have to walk over a mile past the end of the infrequent bus line. Tourists will come, no problem, and they bring in good income for us, but we want to serve folks who wouldn't necessarily get to the garden on their own. So we're looking at putting in a once-a-month free public bus from downtown. But board members disagree about this. It'll be quite expensive for us."

"I'm on the fence about it, at the moment," Margaret volunteered. "We are not a wealthy garden."

She was watching Camila as she cleared the plates. It wasn't a friendly gaze. She sniffed as Camila took her plate. *What in the world has gotten into Margaret? I've never known her to be rude. I wish I'd brought another board member. Why did she want to come, anyway?*

"Kids come on field trips, right?" Hank asked. Bea nodded. "Then there's free public access. Case closed," Hank asserted.

"Well, we'd like families to enjoy it together."

"They can't have everything," Hank answered. Paige blushed.

"Who, exactly are 'they'?" Lila asked coolly.

Camila isn't looking at the floor now. She's watching Lila.

"By 'they,' I mean the general public," Hank said.

"He means 'riffraff,'" Gert said, in a stage whisper.

Camila gave her a quick smile. And Max shifted around in his seat.

"We can discuss all this at length tomorrow. Hank, would you like to state our issue?" Paige said quickly.

Why is she deferring to him? I stated the issue for our garden. She needs to make sure these board members don't consider her a wall decoration. Not a trophy wife, but a trophy executive director.

Hank sat back in his chair and picked up a knife to emphasize his points. "We have a couple of issues. We're going to shrink the lawn and put in low-water-use landscaping... we do know that there are water issues here... but some of us want to avoid native plants, which frankly aren't that... spectacular. But there's another problem, too." At this point in his narrative he began banging his knife to emphasize each point. "We have a 'conditional use permit' from our neighborhood. We can't have more than forty visitors at a time. As you can see, we have a parking problem." This statement was followed by two rapid bangs, which made Bea's butter knife clatter on her plate. "A small lot, and plenty of surfers grabbing the street parking. On weekends we offer valet parking, ten dollars extra for folks who can't walk very far from a parking space. But we need to have events here. A gala." The gala rated significant knife percussion. Paige moved her coffee cup away from her plate. "How can we do that and stay friends with our neighbors?"

Max sat up a little straighter. He wore a serious look. "That's an issue."

"Yes, there's board disagreement about that," Paige cut in. "How about your garden, Lila?"

But Lila had something to say first. "My family's been in real estate for generations. I'll bet there were covenants in this neighborhood until fairly recently?"

"We're long past that kind of prejudice, my dear, although I admit that it was quite exclusive when I first moved here," Max said in his courtly way.

"Just white folks, right?" Gert asked.

"Well, yes, but as I said, we're well past that now."

Camila was refilling Paige's water glass. Her face showed nothing. Paige said, "Yes, we've made quite a bit of progress since then."

"Oh!" she exclaimed, as Camila spilled a little water on the tablecloth.

"So sorry. Let me get you a cloth," Camila said.

"Don't bother. I can use my napkin." This was said kindly, or so it seemed. *Am I imagining this, or did Camila spill water on purpose? What else is going on that I'm not seeing here?*

"Sorry," Camila said again, using her apron to soak up the spill.

"No problem," Paige responded automatically. She was clearly ready to change the subject. "Well, Gert, would you like to state your problem?"

Why is it that having Gert state the problem doesn't seem like a big deal to me, but it did when Paige turned things over to her board member? Probably because Lila can take the job or leave it. Paige is just starting her career.

"Well, we sure as hell don't have a valet service," Gert began. "And we ain't charging $20 admission like I read about in your brochure. We're startin' at $1.00. Our 'conflict' is that Lila here thinks we need more people on our board to carry the load, and I think we're doin' just fine at three of us."

"How do you pay Lila when you're only charging $1.00 admission? Is your garden endowed?" Hank asked.

"Not so well endowed as Mr. Botanist thinks Paige is," Gert said. "And beyond that, it's none of your beeswax."

"Yes, well, again, we can discuss all this tomorrow," said their hostess, whose blush had crept all the way to the top of her forehead. "*I* think it's time we brought some coffee and tea into the living room to listen to Dr. Ramos."

CHAPTER FIVE

After everyone had availed themselves of one of the downstairs bathrooms—the one Bea went to had a shell theme, with shell-shaped soaps, shells on towels and even under glass on a little table—they convened in the living room to hear Armando pontificate. Bea briefly considered pleading that she needed to call to wish her kids good night, but she'd called already that day, and Paige looked like she needed some moral support. Margaret was sitting on the edge of her chair, shooting Paige a disapproving look. Armando was openly admiring her body, which was tastefully displayed in a long lavender linen dress and a matching, form-fitting jacket. Clearly Hank didn't agree with this water conservation stuff, and he was the board president. Bea supposed she could sit through an Armando-lecture one more time in her life, and the fireworks might be interesting.

She almost always agreed with Armando's messages; it was just the messenger himself whom she found repellent. She'd even let that prejudice lead her to think that he was behind a violent attack on her boss at Shandley a few years ago, and some stalking incidents that involved her own family.

Armando started off with a PowerPoint presentation of some pictures from the San Diego region that to Bea, at least, were shocking.

"Note the water trickling down a street from someone's irrigation system; note that the curb is algae-filled, implying a long-term problem."

"Yikes," Bea said.

"This mansion is in Rancho Santa Fe. Note the acres of lawns, citrus and avocado trees." Hank gave Armando a sharp look.

The next slide was a table: San Diego Water had nearly 100 customers who used over a million gallons a year, as opposed to about 31,000 for the average San Diego home.

"Guess they do it because they can," Gert snorted.

Armando then launched into the fact that there was no such thing as a year that did not require water conservation. "San Diego's water is dependent upon snowpack in the Sierra Nevada and the northern Rockies. Just because there is a good snow every year or two, the long-term trend requires a *lot* more conservation! La Jolla Gardens is uniquely positioned to deliver that message!"

Paige scribbled notes as if his word were gospel. Hank was turning red again.

Then Armando launched into something that caused Max to sit up straight again. His face was impassive. "This garden needs to demonstrate to the public the incredible role that native plants play in our world of rapidly decreasing species diversity. Native plants are more than just water conserving plants. They attract native wildlife, and their role in attracting pollinators makes them essential to the continuance of lots of species! I could give a whole talk on this, and I'd be happy to, another time."

Bea clapped loudly after the presentation. It felt good to do so with sincerity. Lila and Gert joined her, but Hank was scowling. Margaret looked like she needed to go to bed. Max clapped faintly and maintained his inscrutability. Paige was stealing glances at her angry board member.

"I don't know if you put in pictures of that Rancho Santa Fe home on purpose, because you know those people are neighbors and dear friends of our family," Hank barked.

Armando did not answer this challenge directly. "All the more reason for La Jolla Gardens to model proper conservation behavior. People like that may take notice," He followed this statement with a definitive nod to Hank.

"You have a lot of nerve, buddy." Hank turned his head towards Paige and rolled his eyes. Margaret caught Bea's eye and rolled *her* eyes. *Where is she in all this? Is she just reacting to the breach in decorum?*

Paige was twisting her hands, and had opened her mouth to say something, but Gert beat her to it. "You old boys fightin' over water or over Paige, now? Looks like both. How 'bout we take a break and come back here for some of my delicious mesquite/prickly pear mead? Might sweeten you up a tad."

"I don't need anything more to drink, thanks," Bea said. "I'll just head upstairs. I need to call home."

"Same here," said Lila.

"I need to head back to my house," Margaret said. "Thanks for an enlightening evening." This was directed to Armando, not her hostess. And it didn't *sound* sarcastic.

"Same here," Hank said. "See you in the morning." He had regained his gallant demeanor. He gave Margaret and Paige both pecks on the cheek and took Margaret's arm as they headed to the lobby. From the living room, Bea watched him hold open the front door for Margaret. She headed towards a silver station wagon parked right in front of the door. Max followed her. "This is a late night for me. My driver's probably more than ready to head home." Hank followed him out.

After Hank closed the door behind them, Paige motioned to Bea to follow her into the kitchen. "I'm truly glad you came. Could I grab you for a just a minute? There's something I'd like to run by you before you turn in." Her confident, hospitable manner had disappeared. She was pulling on the fingers of her left hand. Bea's eyes went from Paige's hands to her eyes. They beseeched her. Bea was vaguely aware of Camila a few feet away, dish towel in hand, immobilized, openly staring at them. Paige didn't seem to mind that she was listening. Or was it that Camila was simply wallpaper?

"Sure, I'd be happy to chat now, Paige, and I'm always up for a walk for a longer talk later," Bea said.

"Thanks." Paige went out through the swinging kitchen doors. "Goodnight, Lila! See you in the morning! And Gert, I'd be happy to try your drink, although I hardly need more alcohol." The hostess persona was back.

Bea followed her out and Paige said, "Bea, if you don't mind, let's talk in the office." Bea felt eyes on her as she followed her hostess to the first-floor room. Judging by the silence, it was several pairs of eyes.

Paige propelled her into a lovely wood-paneled office with floor-to-ceiling books on two walls… lots of field guides and travel books, Bea noticed. The desk was solid oak and so were the file cabinets. There were photos of La Jolla Gardens… fog creeping through primeval-looking cycads, hummingbirds pollinating brilliant California fuchsia bushes, huge waves crashing below the clifftop. There were also photographs of some exotic locations. Bea recognized Machu Picchu and Angkor Wat. One whole set of shelves held carved Oaxacan figures—brightly colored coyotes, dolphins, fish, and lizards, and an assortment of lovely objects like rose quartz crystals, blocks of polished dark blue lapis lazuli, and petrified wood, its inner rings turned to lavender and oranges.

"This was our founder's private office. Mine now." A big pile of files was spread out on the desk, covering Paige's computer. She scooped them up and pulled out a key from under a wooden hand-cranked music box on the desk.

"What a beautiful work," Bea said, as she ran her finger over the music box's intricately intertwined carved wooden animals, probably from some Bavarian forest.

"Were all of these things here, or have you added some of your own?"

"Oh, I've added a thing or two," Paige said as she crammed the files into the front of a very full file cabinet drawer and locked it.

"Interesting place to keep a key." Bea was still fascinated by the wolves, wild boars and roe deer on the music box.

"Yeah, well, I move the key around. You just never know, do you. You're never really sure about people." She put the key back under a large ammonite fossil. "But I'm not worried about a fellow banana slug. It's a bond, don't you think?"

Bea laughed at this reference to their days at UC Santa Cruz, whose mascot was no powerful predator, but a huge bright yellow land slug, whose "Gandhi-like" qualities fit the student body's ideals.

Paige leaned forward. "So, Bea… I'm going to need some time alone with you. Some issues have come up that I don't really want to discuss in the big group. Can we take a walk together first thing Sunday morning?"

"Of course, Paige. I'll help if I can."

"Thanks! It's so good to have peers. This job has been more… challenging… than I expected it to be. And I hear you've had some of your own challenges at Shandley, right? Even murder, although thank God that's not my issue here." She managed a laugh.

Bea decided to take a light tone. "At times it's been plenty challenging. What did we say before we had that euphemism?"

Paige gave a real smile. "Burdensome?"

"Grim? Appalling? How about absolutely awful?"

Paige chortled, but then her expression sobered. "I'm just not sure I'm cut out for this."

"You mean the responsibility of being an executive director?"

"That and... everything." Paige said this while staring at the floor. Suddenly she jerked her head up and pasted on a smile that Bea recognized as her mother's go-to expression when she didn't want to delve into something painful. It was a tactic that Bea had been known to employ, as well.

"Paige, I'm more than happy to help however I can."

Paige got up from the desk and gave Bea a real hug and hung on for a few moments. It was the only time they'd ever been this intimate. "I knew you'd understand, Bea. Sleep well."

"You, too, Paige. It's always more harrowing being the host of something like this. I'm just along for the ride. What a beautiful spot! You're doing well so far," Bea said. Paige's shoulders relaxed a bit.

"I guess I should rejoin the other guests," Paige said, with a sigh. Bea followed her out the office door and watched her return to the fray with real concern. She pasted on that phony smile as she answered a question from Gert. Well, there was nothing more Bea could do tonight, unfortunately. She'd soon find out what was bothering Paige.

She'd watch Paige's dealings with Hank closely. She went back out to say good night to Armando and Gert, who had cognac glasses full of mead. Paige waved a wistful goodbye. *Wistful because she wishes she were heading up the stairs, too.* Bea waved to them all and went through the swinging doors to the kitchen to say good night to Camila. She was scrubbing fish skin off a baking sheet.

"Thanks, Camila. I'll bet you're at least as ready for bed as I am," Bea said.

Camila gave her a frank look. "Yes."

Bea looked at the other door leading out of the kitchen. "Wow, a separate entrance to the kitchen. Like Gert said, very Downton Abbey."

"Yes." That was all Camila was going to say.

"See you in the morning."

"Yes."

What a successful interaction.

Bea mounted the dramatic staircase. It was not possible to be inconspicuous in this house. She waved from the landing, *like some queen, for God's sake.* Armando was refilling his glass. *I hope Paige feels like she can head to bed before they finish drinking.*

Bea disappeared into her luxury suite and considered her calls. It was too late to call home, even though Arizona, which didn't change back and forth from daylight savings time, was now in the same time zone as California. But Frank at his conference in northern California would be up, she hoped.

He picked up right away.

"First of all, I miss you," she said. "Secondly, coming here may have been a big mistake."

"How so?"

"Well, Paige and her board president seem to be locked in a major disagreement about the direction of La Jolla Gardens. I think she invited us all here to back her up. But we're not going to change this guy's mind. At any rate, she's very upset about something, and we're going to talk about it Sunday morning. Then, to make matters worse, the board member I brought along—you remember that was Margaret, because she asked to come—has some beef with Paige from the looks of it. Supposedly she's old friends with Paige's parents. Then Armando Ramos showed up to be the after-dinner speaker, if you can believe it. And Paige gets to have *him* as a new board member, lucky her."

Frank burst out into a deep laugh. She could imagine his whole body shaking. "Absolutely your favorite person, I know. The only thing that worries me about him is that murders seem to follow him around. Although the same thing could be said about you."

“Thanks a lot, sweetie. So… how was your day?

“Far less exciting than yours. We’re basically learning how to fill out new forms. But let me tell you about the walk I took through the forest. Spectacular.”

Bea felt considerably better listening to his familiar voice describe a tunnel of overhanging California oaks leading to a small stream.

“Okay, maybe I’m being overly dramatic about all this, Frank.”

They said tender goodbyes, and Frank ended with, “Sleep well. And enjoy the beach, if not the company.”

CHAPTER SIX

Bea had a restless night. She never did well in a new bed, luxury accommodation or not. But that wasn't really it. She'd felt increasingly uneasy as the evening progressed. The group was splintered, sharp little pieces sticking out everywhere. Frank's jokes about murder hadn't helped either. Bea woke up from a dream of trying to surf, falling off a surfboard, and getting caught under it—and hearing a cry nearby from a fellow surfer. She lay still in the night, glancing at a digital clock for the time. Just after one in the morning. No sounds coming from anywhere. She managed to return to sleep, waking early.

Breakfast wasn't until 7:30, so she pulled on her jeans and jacket and shivered her way out into the morning fog. She walked through the gardens first, noticing the dew on every blade of grass, and on the big pom-poms of the South African proteas. The fog was chilly but somehow soothing. Maybe it was because she was a desert creature, always drawn to moisture. This coast might not get as much annual rainfall as the Sonoran Desert, but the dew surely helped lots of things grow here.

A security guard ambled up to her. Her eyes slid to his firearm. He wasn't touching it, thank God.

"You a guest here?" he asked. She looked into his acne-scarred young face. *He can't be much past high-school age. Maybe ex-military.* A red plastic name tag declared that his name was Ace. His white uniform shirt was a little tight across the belly, and there were mustard stains in the same area.

"Hi, Ace. Yes, I'm a guest here… Bea Rivers. I'm out for a walk before breakfast."

"Yeah, it seems like everybody on this guest list likes to take walks at all hours."

"Oh, really?"

"Yeah. Look!" He consulted a paper tucked into his pocket, as he checked off her name and the time, 6:30 AM. She got a brief look at check marks by Paige, Gert, Armando, and Camila. She didn't really catch the times, but she assumed they were from the night before.

"Well, I'm glad you're keeping an eye on things, Ace."

He relaxed a little then. He was so young. "Thanks, ma'am. You're a lot more polite than some of the others."

"Oh?"

"Well, that Camila's a case. Walking around in the middle of the night. She's an illegal, you know. And that Armando is just plain mean." *This is a little much first thing in the morning. Although he's not wrong about Armando.*

Ace put the list back in his pocket, saying "Have a nice walk." He wandered off. Bea glanced back at him and saw his thumbs racing across his phone.

Musical trills and loud squawks emanated from the aviary. Standing in the gazebo, Bea saw that she and the birds were by no means the first ones up and out in this neighborhood. A couple of dozen surfers rode the waves, little black dots she could barely see through the fog. She shivered and remembered her dream. She'd take a brisk walk before she had to return to their motley group.

Cruising by the mansions, some of them Colonial, some huge-windowed modern structures no doubt designed by some famous architect, Bea felt truly chilled now. An ambulance sped by; had a surfer had an accident in the huge waves? Luxury cars headed out of the neighborhood, and Ace went by on a motorcycle, off shift at 7:00, no doubt. The neighborhood security guard in his SafeT Security Services car slowed as he passed her. Bea waved, and he returned the favor. Up at the top of the street, she saw a city bus let out three Latinas. She suspected they were coming in for a day of housekeeping or nannying. She doubted that many neighborhood residents took the bus.

The only other people she saw were barefoot surfers, unloading their boards from roof racks, then racing towards the road down to the beach. She thought of following them from these sandstone cliffs that housed all the mansions and their spectacular views. *They must be three hundred feet above the beach.* But she didn't want to be late for breakfast. Not that she was hungry; she just felt a responsibility towards Paige, towards helping her make some kind of success of this gathering. Bea had dragged Margaret, Lila, and Gert here, and she owed them, too.

Hank pulled up in his black Jaguar just as Bea reached the front door. He looked chipper in his polo shirt and Top-siders: all traces of last night's drunken anger had left his face.

"I'm looking forward to this!" he said. "Let's have fun!"

Okay, if this is the way it's going to be, it could be an okay day.

Margaret pulled up in the Mercedes that she'd called her "La Jolla wagon."

She seemed cheerful today, too. "It's a beautiful new day. As my mother used to say, let's keep it that way."

So far, so good.

The three of them walked into the dining room. Camila was setting out plates of scrambled eggs. Blueberry muffins, bacon, and cantaloupe were in crystal bowls, ready to be passed around. Gert had begun to eat, but Lila and Armando sat politely in front of their plates.

"Paige with you?" Armando asked.

"No," Bea said, "she's probably in the kitchen."

Camila came out with the coffeepot and shook her head.

"I'm sure she'll be here in a minute. Since everybody else is here, how about if we eat our eggs before they get cold," Lila said, stealing a glance at her board member's quickly emptying plate.

It was much like any breakfast in a B and B where the people don't know each other all that well and aren't fully awake enough to be clever. Armando tried the joke about botanists sending mail through the compost office, but when Hank glared at him, he applied himself to a second muffin.

"I need to get going, but I sure would like to thank our hostess," he said.

"Bet you would," Gert mumbled with a mouth full of bacon.

"I'll see if I can find her," Bea offered. "Maybe she got an important phone call. I'm pretty much done eating."

"I'll check around downstairs if you want to go up to her room," Hank said. He still had a lot of food on his plate, but he seemed concerned. Bea nodded at him, and headed up the winding stairs, once again making a stage exit. She headed to the room at the end of the hall that she'd figured was Paige's.

She called a couple of times before opening the door slowly, expecting to find Paige on the phone, wrapped up in some conversation. But she wasn't there. Bea was dimly aware of walls covered with beautiful photographs and prints, but she stared at the neatly made bed. Had Paige gone out for a walk? Or hadn't she gone to bed? Had she spent the night with a lover? This wasn't like her. She'd been doing a professional job of being a gracious hostess. And she clearly wanted to be seen as a professional executive director, too.

Bea trotted down the stairs, rejoining the others just as Hank showed up.

"She's not in her room, " Bea said, and looked at Hank, who was shaking his head.

"I couldn't find her either." He pursed his lips. He clearly thought she should be representing the Gardens better.

Margaret was shaking her head in a tsk-tsk-y way. Armando raised an eyebrow. Lila murmured, "How odd." Camila didn't seem to be reacting one way or another, but she was good at that. But it was Gert who, as usual, said the hidden part out loud.

"Either she's pretty damned rude, or there's something wrong."

"It doesn't seem in character, does it?" Bea asked.

"Maybe we should take a look around the grounds," Hank suggested.

"Camila, why don't you come with us?" Lila said. Camila nodded and undid her apron.

The group headed out the door near the picture windows, as they'd done for their tour the night before. "I'll go right, towards the proteas and the aviary," Lila said. "I'll join you," said Margaret.

The rest of them headed straight back towards the gazebo. And the edge with the flagging tape. There was a sign there that Bea hadn't noticed before. Horribly, it pictured someone falling down a cliff, with the warning "Stay Back! Unstable cliffs." Hank and Armando gave each other a look and went over the tape almost to the edge of the cliff about three feet beyond it.

Suddenly Bea heard a loud voice. *A bullhorn? Lifeguards had bullhorns...* "Stand back! Stand back from the edge!" The voice was directly underneath them, but Bea couldn't see anything. The cliffs were obscuring that part of the beach.

Armando and Hank stepped back over the flagging tape. "God, maybe part of the cliffs crumbled and crushed somebody. It's happened here before. But usually when it's been raining a lot, and during king tides, but we haven't had either of those lately," Armando said.

"Maybe somebody didn't fall off but was walking down there in the middle of the night..." Camila began.

"And some rocks came down and crushed them?" Bea said.

"Paige knows better than to walk right under the cliffs. We've talked about it. She grew up here. She knows better," Hank said. But he was clenching his jaw as he spoke. He turned in the direction of the aviary and shouted, "Margaret, Lila, sounds like there's been an accident on the beach!"

"Not...?" Margaret shouted back, in a shaky voice.

"We certainly hope not. But we don't know. I guess we can check the rest of the grounds," Hank said, although he seemed as dispirited as Bea was feeling.

The group broke off into twos and threes, looking even in the tool sheds and by the garbage cans off the kitchen. In a few minutes, they all filed into the living room without any clues as to Paige's whereabouts, in time to hear the doorbell. Hank opened the door to a heavy, jowly policeman.

"Sir, I need to speak to someone in charge here."

"I guess that's me."

"Sir, I'm very sorry to tell you that a young woman has fallen from the cliff right behind this house The business card in her pocket identified her as Paige Pearson, Executive Director of La Jolla Gardens. Two detectives will be here shortly. We'd like to ask that all people on the premises to remain here until they arrive." He said this as his head swiveled to take in the group rapidly gathering behind Hank.

"Dear me!" Margaret muttered, and she began to collapse. Hank turned and caught her, then pulled her upright.

"Is she... is she still alive?" Bea asked.

"Ma'am, I hate to say it, but it's pretty much impossible to survive a 300-foot fall," the cop said.

Hank helped Margaret to a chair. Bea headed to a couch. They all seemed to need a seat.

"I will need to stay here until Detective Nguyen arrives." He remained standing.

"Yes, sir. Thank you," Hank said.

Armando asked, "So there was a cliff collapse in the night?"

"The cliff didn't fall, the woman did," the cop said.

"You mean... the cliff didn't give way?"

"That is what I mean." His phone rang and he walked to the foyer, within view of the living room, and talked quietly.

Bea said in a near-whisper, "Well, you said she knew these cliffs well enough that she wouldn't walk right under them, Hank. You said that when we thought maybe she'd been hit by a rockfall down on the beach. Surely she also knew them well enough that she wouldn't go over the flagging tape and slip and fall."

"I would agree with that," he said, equally quietly.

"I also agree with that. I've known her a long time." Camila hesitated. Then she added, "She's been really stressed out."

"You think she'd throw herself off a cliff?" Bea asked, trying to keep her voice soft.

"No. I don't think she would," said Camila.

"Then..." Bea began, but Camila picked up the apron she'd taken off and disappeared into the kitchen.

"Bea, are you about to imply that somebody pushed Paige off a cliff? There were far too many murders at Shandley Gardens when I was there. Don't assume they happen everywhere," Armando said, in the tone he used to employ when he'd been on the Shandley board. Scolding her, as if she were a child, or an underling, instead of a peer his own age. He was not trying to modulate his voice, and the policeman, no longer on his phone, was looking at him curiously as he headed into the living room.

"Armando, I'm as shocked and horrified and confused by this as we all are. Let's be decent to each other, at least."

"Thank you, Bea," Margaret said, with an eye-roll so quick that Bea wasn't entirely sure she'd seen it. Margaret had barely tolerated Armando when they'd been on the board together. "I'm sure this Officer Nin, or whatever his name is, will clear things up soon."

Bea wasn't at all sure about the clearing things up part, but the soon part was right. The doorbell rang again.

CHAPTER SEVEN

Detective Ted Nguyen did not waste his time, or theirs, with niceties. He and another detective, Bob Bingham, had a short talk with Hank in the hallway. Hank, continuing to play host, had answered the doorbell again, but Bea couldn't decipher what he was being asked. He gestured towards them all, already gathered where they'd been enjoying chardonnay just over twelve hours earlier. As the officers approached, Bea crossed her legs the opposite way and noticed others sitting up straighter or coughing. *We're all trying to look as alert and innocent as possible.*

"Everyone in the house is in this room?"

"No," Armando said. "There's someone in the kitchen. I'll get her." He went through the swinging doors and returned with Camila following. She sat next to Bea on the couch. She was twisting her hands and looking at the tiled floor.

The detectives remained standing and faced them. Detective Nguyen was clearly the senior guy. He was small and fit, with a trim mustache, and he spoke slowly, gravely and precisely.

"A young woman named Paige Pearson fell to her death below this facility sometime in the night. The time is yet to be determined by the medical examiner. She died as soon as she hit the beach. You probably would not wish to know the medical details."

Bea shivered.

"We are treating this as a suspicious death. We have

not ruled out accidental death or suicide," he said, continuing in a severe tone. "We understand that she was in charge of this facility, so it is surprising that she would have made the mistake of getting too close to the edge of the cliff. We will be interviewing those who were here last night... which Mr. Archer says includes all of you. He has said that there were also two people who were here last night who are not here this morning, and we will interview them as well." He consulted his notes. "Max Danes and the security guard, Ace Karlsson. Please inform us of any others. I will also be talking to you about Ms. Pearson's state of mind. You may notice that a team will be looking over the grounds and the area from which she fell. Please do not go outdoors while they are working. After that, do not cross the area that we close off. Mr. Archer, is there a room that can be made available for the next couple of days for our use?"

"Well, I supposed the office is best. It's on the ground floor, and I can't imagine we'll need to do any garden business now. In fact, I'd better ask the groundskeeper, who should be arriving any moment, to put up the chain and the 'closed' sign. Oh, no. I don't even know if he works today. I usually ask Paige these things," he muttered.

"And maybe someone should change the voice mail to say that the garden is closed this weekend?" said Bea before she could stop herself. *This is not your garden.*

"Yes, Bea, thank you. Could you help me with that?" Hank asked with a good amount of grace.

And so it began. Bea showed Hank how to change the message, wondering who did this for him at his house. She helped him find the "closed" sign in a garden shed, because the gardener was *not* on duty that day.

She was grateful that she could retreat to her bedroom before she was called, as could the others who'd spent the night there. Officer Bingham got all of their cell numbers and said that they should stay on site until further notice. Hank ushered Margaret into an unused first floor bedroom, next to Camila's. She had something constructive to do; she was back cleaning up breakfast. Hank held down the living room.

Bea called Frank and it went straight to voice mail. He also didn't answer her text. *He told me he'd be pretty unavailable during the day, and they might be out of cell phone range. This is what happens when your husband works for the National Park Service and not in an office.* She called her mother, who was about to get the kids (and her husband) into the car to go to the Desert Museum.

"Honey, I love you dearly, but I do not understand how you can possibly be involved in another murder investigation. Surely they'll let you off the hook and you can still come home tomorrow evening?"

"Surely. God knows I have no motive."

"That's good, because your father is tiring so easily. We're getting him checked out on Monday."

Oh, God, I'm relying on them too much.

"Mother, I'll be home just as soon as I can. Believe me, that's all I want to do right now."

She looked out the window. There seemed to be quite a commotion around the edge of the cliff with the flagging tape. "Damn!" she heard one man shout. "Footprints everywhere! What is this? A group plan to screw up the crime scene?" Another cop clearly told him to shush, and she couldn't distinguish anything else they said. Uniformed people were stringing crime scene tape the entire length of the cliffs, on the house-side of the gazebo.

Her phone buzzed and her attention was diverted. She was to meet Detective Nguyen in the office.

She knocked on the door, and Officer Bingham opened the door to that lovely wood-paneled room. She sat in an oak chair with dark red cushions facing the desk, the officers, and the music box. Seeing that again made her suddenly terribly sad. They'd shared a moment of intimacy, she and Paige, and she'd hoped to help her more that weekend.

Despite her relatively brief tenure—just five years—as a botanical garden professional, this was the third time she'd been questioned about a murder. However, her old friend Marcia Samuelson had been the investigator for both earlier times. Detective Ted Nguyen had no reason to trust her, and he didn't appear to. He looked over his notes before he raised his head and asked her for a detailed account of her whereabouts the previous evening and night. He was watching her very closely She would not be intimidated.

"What time did you leave the gathering in the living room last night?"

"About 10:00... a little after."

"And did you leave your room at any time in the night or early this morning?"

"Not in the night. I did go for a walk around 6:30 this morning."

He scribbled something.

"I spoke with the security guard, Ace. He recorded my walk at 6:30 and had also recorded people who were out on the grounds during his night shift. There were several."

"We have asked him to come in shortly. We understand that you knew Ms. Pearson well?"

"No, not well. We were acquaintances in college more than twenty years ago, and recently discovered that we'd both become executive directors of botanical gardens. She seemed to be having some tensions on her board, and she planned this weekend get-together to get board members and directors to talk over problems. I will say that she seemed very nervous and had planned to talk to me in private about something. I don't know what it was."

"Could she have been depressed enough to take her own life?"

"My gut reaction is no. But I *really* didn't know her

that well, and we never got a chance to have a good talk. She did mention something about if I wondered if it was all worth it, and when I asked if she meant being an executive director, it seemed like maybe there was more to it. But she was vague, and I just don't know how far her discomfort went. I don't know if she was truly depressed. I wish I could give you a clearer answer."

He dismissed her, eventually, and told her to call him if she thought of anything. Since the weekend workshop was supposed to last until Sunday afternoon, he was asking all out-of-town participants to stay in San Diego until then. More than 24 hours more. Which meant that Bea would stay in her luxury accommodations, which were feeling quite a bit more claustrophobic than they had the night before. *On the other hand, maybe I can help figure out what happened. I was useful the other times.*

"I hope you solve this soon," she said to Nguyen.

"We will," he responded.

Bea trudged up the dramatic staircase. She suddenly had time on her hands. She felt like she'd had almost no down time since Andy was born ten years ago. Having kids and working, then being a single mom and working, then being the director, where the buck stopped... and still raising kids... well, it certainly didn't lend itself to leisure time.

She could work on a grant. *No! That's the wrong way to use this time!* She could walk on the beach. *Better idea.* She could seek out Lila for that. Lila steadied her. Or... she could find Camila. There was something odd going on with her. She used to work for Paige's parents. She said she knew Paige pretty well. Margaret didn't like Camila. And despite the fact that Camila seemed like a possible "suspect"—if this was indeed murder, which please Lord, it was not—Bea had some sympathy for her. She was playing the dutiful "Downton Abbey" role that Gert had called out and playing it with resentment that not everyone seemed to notice. There was more to Camila than met the eye.

Bea knocked on the door of Camila's room near the kitchen. The office door down the hall was closed, and the acoustics in the mansion were such that Bea figured Detective Nguyen couldn't hear their conversation. "Come in," Camila called. She was on her laptop. She closed it abruptly when Bea walked in.

"Camila," Bea began, "if you have a minute, I want to ask you about Paige."

Camila nodded cautiously, her eyes searching Bea's.

"Thanks. Well, we both agree Paige wouldn't accidentally walk on the cliff edge. Surely the fog wasn't *that* disorienting. Was Paige really distressed enough to jump?" Bea stopped and looked down at her hands, then leveled her gaze. "Do you think somebody could have pushed her?"

Camila turned her desk chair to face Bea and gestured for her to sit in the armchair. "Why are you coming to me with this?" *She* didn't trust Bea; unlike Ted Nguyen, Camila didn't camouflage her thoughts.

Bea saw no reason to dissemble. "Because you have a history with her. Your parents worked for her parents. You know her."

"Yes, I've known her all my life."

"I feel terrible that Paige came to this end and I'd like to help figure out what happened to her. And I... well, I thought maybe we could think things through together."

Camila stared at her for what felt like a full minute. Without that ridiculous uniform on, beside her laptop and in jeans, she looked like a student at the nearby university. Maybe a graduate student.

She finally sighed and said, "Okay, Bea, I could use an ally here. There's a lot to my history with Paige, which worries me in this situation. Besides that awful sexist Armando, I'm the only one with brown skin. You know, the butler did it."

"Yeah." Bea held her gaze.

"Okay, here's the deal. My parents worked for the Pearsons for thirty years. My mom was the cook and housekeeper, and my dad did everything outdoors. They also helped Margaret and her husband out when they came from Tucson in the summers. I actually grew up in a small house on the grounds of the Pearson mansion. Paige and I are the same age, and we used to play together, until her mother started to discourage it. Paige defied her until the girls at her private school clearly did *not* think it was cool to play with me, so she dropped me."

"Sorry," Bea said, although it seemed a wholly inadequate response.

"Don't be. It was good training for 'the slings and arrows of outrageous fortune."' Camila's lips pursed in amusement as Bea raised her eyebrows.

"Well, I *did* go to La Jolla High, which required reading lots of Shakespeare. And UCSD, where I got a sociology degree in December. And I hope to go to law school if the Dream Act passes. I was born in Oaxaca."

Bea took all of this in. Camila looked at her computer for a minute. *She's trying to decide whether to tell me something.*

"I feel a little sorry for Paige. She never has been able to figure out who she is. I think deep down she's still the kid that played "girl explorers" with me, when we discovered new islands that no boy had ever seen. But then there's the pull of her parents, of the people she grew up with. Of the powerful men she grew up with. Paige is a person without true friends, in my opinion."

Bea nodded and considered this. "So what does Margaret have against you?"

"Ah." Camila folded the hands in her lap. She was still looking directly at Bea. "I haven't told you the rotten part of the story. My mom got cancer, and couldn't work, and my dad had to take care of her, so he eventually couldn't work much. Of course they had no health insurance, much less disability. And they definitely did not have the beneficence of their employers. They were fired and evicted from the cottage on the grounds. They were living with relatives when there was a raid. They got deported back to a place they hadn't lived for 30 years, destitute and, in my mom's case, deathly ill. She died shortly afterwards, and my father has been inconsolable. I've found a lawyer to sue the Pearsons, but my dad may well be dead if and when it ever comes to court."

Camila blew out an angry breath, and Bea exhaled for the first time during this little speech.

"So Margaret doesn't appreciate the fact that you're suing her friends?"

"No. And Paige took her parents' part in the fight. It's not just that blood is thicker than water... it's a whole culture here that our lawsuit is challenging. It's Paige's tribe."

"I'm surprised she offered you this weekend job. And that you took it."

"I need the money. That's why I took it. As to why she offered it... I have no idea. Guilt, maybe? We really were close as children."

"What a mess. I can see why you'd be concerned about being a suspect."

"Yes. So what are you going to do with this information?"

"I'll leave it up to you what you tell Ted Nguyen. You haven't seen him yet?"

"Nope. In," she checked her watch, "a couple of hours. I'm sure he's going to interview the Pearsons, and they have many friends in high places. Including the chief of police. They will probably implicate me."

"Unless it's ruled an accident or a suicide. What do you think about Paige throwing herself off the cliff?"

"Well, something was bothering her. When we met

about me doing the gig this weekend, she was checking her phone every couple of minutes, and she wasn't looking forward to whatever it was she was looking for. There are some power players on that board, and I wouldn't be surprised if she was out of her depth."

"Is putting in more native plants and saving water so controversial that it would spark this much drama?"

"Bea, I grew up around these people. I helped serve them at parties, just like I did last night. They expect to get their way. Period."

"Wow. Yikes. Well, if there's anything I can do to help you out, let me know."

"Thanks. I need to get back to these law school applications. If you can help get the Dream Act passed, that would be good."

Bea laughed and touched Camila on the shoulder as she said, "Thank you. Thank you for telling me about all of this. It's a tough story."

Camila just nodded.

As she left, the office door opened, and Gert emerged, scowling. "Have fun with that one," she said, and breezed by. Bea wondered if Ted Nguyen was one of those neat-and-trim people who disdain people with wild hair and dirty fingernails. Gert hadn't done much to make herself presentable, which shouldn't matter, but...

She decided to find Lila for that beach walk. Lila said she'd love to talk things over before *she* was interviewed, at 4:00, but would Bea mind if Gert came along? "She flung open the door on the way back from talking to the cops and was pretty furious with me that I'd 'dragged her over here.' I gather that things did not go well."

The three women headed down the paved road to the beach, the same road Bea had watched early that morning, when all had been right with the world. Surfers were striding up the steep hill with surfboards under their arms, all in wetsuits, some unzipped to the waist. Bea pulled her sweater tighter; the morning fog had not lifted. Lila and Gert zipped their jackets.

"I'll be glad to get home. Too many people here and it's too damn humid! *And* cold," Gert declared.

"Shh," Bea said. "Look at the brittlebush! Same yellow daisy-like flowers as our desert brittlebush, but this one's got greener leaves. A coastal variety. Those poppies are close to our desert versions, too. This one's just a different subspecies; it's a little bigger, but the same gorgeous golden orange color. And those purple scorpionweeds... see they look like scorpion tails... they grow everywhere."

"Even Copperton," Lila said.

"Wow, look at the wild buckwheat! Those pink-and-white flowers are gorgeous! I think those guys are crazy not to want native plants in La Jolla Gardens!"

"And look at these weird succulents. They look like they're from South Africa or something. What the heck are they, Bea?" Lila asked.

"They're dudleyas. Liveforevers. Also natives here. They can live with very little soil and in harsh environments, up to 100 years. English explorers were shocked that dudleyas survived the sea voyages back to England pressed between the pages of their books. Look, that one's in bloom! Long stalk with red flowers, see? Isn't it cool with that little basal rosette?"

"Well, Miss Goody Two Shoes, are you looking at all the rocks on this road? Seems like these cliffs sure enough fall down."

"Yeah, I can't argue with you about that, Gert." Bea said with less enthusiasm. She saw that small round rocks held together some of the sandstone above them. A few had fallen into the road. "Looks like some of the surfers are making their own trails down from the top. Shortcuts to the road."

"Not real smart," Gert said.

They got to the bottom of the road and turned north,

in the direction of Paige's cliff fall. Bea got a good view of the cliffs. Some of them were nearly sheer; others not so steep, with a couple of little canyons running through them. There were sharp sandstone turrets near the top, and below those, large boulders and piles of sand had fallen.

"So, right before we left, when I was checking out La Jolla, I found a video online of those cliffs collapsing a couple of years ago." Lila said.

Bea nodded. "Yeah, Armando mentioned that, too. We'd better stay out towards the water."

They were forced towards the water anyway, as there was plenty of crime scene tape at the base of the cliffs.

"See, we figured that out right away. I don't think Paige needed her whole life here to figure out she shouldn't be walkin' under those cliffs. I'm guessin' she can read," Gert said, gesturing to a sign that showed a crumbling cliff and another sign that proclaimed "Danger!"

"Yeah, I agree," Lila said. "And the wet sand's so much easier to walk on down here. Hard packed." She turned away from the cliffs towards the sea. "Those surfers are so graceful."

Surfers were cresting enormous waves.

"Crazy," Gert muttered. "Like everybody at this meeting you hauled me to, Lila. Including the cops. How did you two do with them?"

"Not much to report," Lila said.

"Me neither," Bea added.

"Well, I got something to report, or anyway, the cops think I do," Gert complained. "The cops dug up that old deal about us buying stolen pottery from Indian graves... you remember that, Bea... and you know we were not charged. Which I told them, and that Nguyen guy looked like he thought I was lying!" Gert kicked a small rock out of their path. "*Then* they mentioned some old assault-and-battery charge." This time she kicked away an empty plastic water bottle.

"What assault-and-battery charge?" Lila had stopped dead in her tracks.

"There was two of 'em. I was in my twenties and thirties, dang it. Didn't you do dumb stuff then, too?"

"Some."

Bea looked over at Lila, who was rubbing her forehead. Bea suspected that Lila's transgressions during those decades were not of the violent kind.

They were silent for a while. Bea was watching some sandpipers nodding along and then plunging their beaks into the sand to retrieve something delicious. She decided not to mention them to avoid another caustic "goody two shoes" accusation from Gert. But Gert interrupted anyway, bursting out with "And somebody told them I was 'hostile' to Paige last night! Can you believe the nerve! Who's tellin' on me! Lucky for you two I don't think it's you."

Bea agreed with that statement. She stole another glance at Lila, who frowned and gave Gert a long look. *Is she wondering if Gert is more dangerous than she appears? Or just if she's likely to cause problems for their garden?*

There was another silence, broken only by the crunching of tiny shells beneath their feet. Bea decided to try to break the tension between her two companions by venturing out into the surf with her water sandals and rolled-up pants. The water reached to mid-calf until a particularly big wave rolled in, soaking her to the tops of her thighs. "Lord, that's cold!"

"So I gotta tell you gals somethin' else," Gert said, continuing to be oblivious to the joys of southern California. "I couldn't sleep last night, and I took a walk then, to look at the stars, which, by the way, you can't see, because of all these clouds. But anyhoo, I was halfway out that lawn when I ran into that pimple-faced guard, and he asked what I was doing, and I told him just what it looked like—I couldn't sleep and I needed to take a walk. But a few minutes after I went inside, I thought I heard a scream."

Bea gulped. "What time was that?"

"Oh, maybe one o'clock. I thought somebody was having a nightmare; I didn't pay it much mind."

"I assume the guard will report that," Bea said.

"He's in there talkin' to them right now," Gert said. "I don't trust him."

"Why not?" Bea asked.

"Call it my woman's intuition," was all Gert would say.

Another period of quiet followed this comment.

"Look at this kelp," Bea said, pulling on a four-foot-long piece of seaweed with a ball in the middle. "I think this round thing is filled with air and holds the kelp up in the sea."

"Stinks," Gert said.

Lila rolled her eyes.

"I'll head up. Wonder when they'll let us go home?" Gert turned back towards the road. Bea sighed. She fully intended to walk for at least an hour; the tide was out far enough for that, even if it *was* coming in (she realized she should have checked the tide tables online). She and Lila stopped to watch surfers catch enormous waves. They stayed upright until they disappeared under the waves, resurfacing to swim ashore with their boards. Both women wandered in and out of the chilly water, taking care to do so between waves. Their feet tingled as they scuffed through the wet sand; then they'd head up to the dry sand to warm up. A seal's head bobbed up every so often; he was swimming north faster than they could walk. Bea took huge gulps of sea air, and with each deep breath she relaxed a little. "I see why everybody from Tucson and Phoenix flocks here. Especially later in the year, when it's still cool here and it's horribly hot in the desert."

"Yup. The cab driver called you guys Zonies. At least

there aren't enough New Mexicans here to call us Newmies or something."

They passed a lifeguard station with high and low tides filled in on a board with red marker. As well as the water temperature. "No wonder our toes are so cold! The water's fifty-eight degrees!" Lila said.

Then she noticed something before Bea did. They'd gotten to a place on the beach where dogs were no longer allowed. Apparently, this was also the place where clothing was optional. The first few deeply tanned nudists were all single males, clearly displaying their wares to passers-by. It was time to turn around. *Let's keep this beach walk simple. This day is complicated enough.*

On the way up the steep hill, Bea was glad she was used to Tucson's over 2,500-foot elevation. She wasn't wheezing her way up this sea-level challenge. And without Gert, she could exclaim about the aroma of the coastal sagebrush. "Clean and clear and soothing at the same time." But they were both glad for a stop at the viewpoint halfway up. It *was* a steep road, although the surfers running swiftly up it, carrying surfboards, belied that fact.

They stood and watched a couple of people fishing off kayaks out beyond the breakers. That took a little more skill than sitting on the bank of a lake. A group of swimmers was out there, too... a school of red swim caps.

"There are a lot of really good athletes here," Lila observed. "Is it a residence requirement?"

"The Pacific Ocean is a misnomer. You have to be skilled to enjoy it," Bea said. "So, Lila..."

"Yeah?"

"You don't really suspect Gert, do you?"

"Probably not. But I don't doubt her ability to get herself or our garden into hot water."

"Well, yeah."

They made it to the top of the hill and ambled back to the house, noting the neighborhood Jaguars and the surfers' ancient vans. They'd been gone an hour and a half. On the way to their respective rooms, she and Lila made plans for dinner. There were going to catch a cab to downtown La Jolla for some fresh seafood, damn the costs.

Back in her room, Bea turned on her computer and pretended to ignore the work-related emails, which she'd forwarded automatically to her personal account. *That was stupid of me.* She saw enough to know that there was nothing that needed her attention right now. She sighed with relief, preparing to do a little investigation of the people she found herself with in La Jolla. But just then her phone rang. It was Angus's cell phone. So much for forgetting about Shandley Gardens for a bit.

"Hey, Angus."

"Never a dull moment, boss."

"Cut out the 'boss' business. What's up?"

"Francie quit. She's on for tomorrow, so I've got to come in."

"Why'd she quit?"

"The curse of the brides. This one brought a dog, in direct conflict with our contract. Francie told her the dog wasn't allowed. The bride argued with her, and meanwhile the pooch dug up a penstemon. Really nice one, by the way. Guess there was something interesting underneath. Anyway, Francie lost it, the woman started crying and told her she was ruining her wedding, and Francie quit. Effective immediately."

"It sounds like if it wasn't this incident, it would've been another. Sorry you have to come in on Saturday."

"Me, too. I have a feeling there will be a lot of clean up after this shindig."

"Is the dog out of the picture now?"

"Yeah, the groom called somebody to come get him. The groom seemed pretty teed off with the bride. Not sure if this will be the wedding for the ages."

"This isn't the beach vacation for the ages, either. I'll tell you about it when I get home."

"Okay, boss."

Bea tried calling Frank again. Straight to voice mail. *He's out having fun in the field.* Just then, a call came in from her home landline.

Maybe it's just the kids wanting to say hello.

"Mom," Andy's voice declared as only a 10-year-old could, "Grandma said I could call."

"I miss you, sweetie."

"I miss you, too. But that's not why I'm calling. I talked to Dad today. He says there's no way I can quit Little League."

Just what I need, another conflict with my ex-husband.

Andy wanted to quit because his coach was a bully. Their team always lost, and instead of giving them a pep talk, the kids had to run ten laps around the field after the games. It hadn't gotten really hot yet, but Bea thought this kind of behavior could be life-threatening in a few weeks. She'd talked to another mom who'd withdrawn her kid because she heard the coach had insisted on punitive laps in 105-degree weather. Bea intended to sit down and talk to the coach with Frank.

"I'll talk to your dad. But first I need to talk to Coach Bradley."

"Dad says I can't act like a sissy."

"You are not a sissy. You are a smart, caring, fun little boy whom I love very much. We'll work this out."

"Thanks, Mom." A suppressed sniffle.

"Have fun with Grandma and Grandpa. You don't get to see them much."

"Okay. I love you, Mom."

"Me, too. Is your sister around?"

"Oh, she's out in the yard playing ball with Joe from next door."

"Give her a hug for me."

After she got off the phone, Bea felt like heading home immediately, professionalism be damned. But Andy would have a fine time with his grandparents, and she was clearly not able to leave even if she wanted to.

If she had to be here, she might as well try to figure out what was going on. She went into the bathroom, washed her face with cold water and some sort of lavender luxury soap, and opened her laptop.

What about this Ace guy. I wonder if there's anything to Gert's "woman's intuition?" She googled Ace Karlsson. Somehow, she had remembered the guy's last name. After a lot of scrolling, she found a blog with a home page photo of a young guy surrounded by a couple of dozen guns. He was taking aim at the camera. She stared at the picture. It had to be him. Same short, stocky build, same super-short brown hair. Same bad skin. And posters behind him about "Sunny San Diego" *and* "Down with the Elites!" with a picture of a building blowing up.

Did he think Paige was an 'elite'? Her family fit the definition.

A recent post complained about how his 'elite' employer should have given him a big tip, but "she never did an honest day's work in her life."

And then there were some posts about how immigrants were swarming over the border and taking jobs like his as a security guard. *I doubt there are many non-citizen security guards. Unless they have green cards.*

He'd served in Iraq. Pictures of him with war buddies, all with guns.

Did the rest of their weekend group need to worry about getting offed by an "elite"-hater? Hank would certainly qualify. And Margaret. And Max. And Ace had called Camila an "illegal."

She'd told Detective Nguyen she'd let him know if she thought of anything. She called and left a message. He was still interviewing, no doubt.

CHAPTER EIGHT

BEA HEADED DOWN TO THE kitchen to see what she could find in the fridge. That was what she'd tell anybody who came by, and she found a can of fizzy water to back up her story. But she lingered in the living room, so she could see who was coming in and out of the office. Sure enough, her buddy Armando stormed out, and he was *not* amused to find her watching his exit.

"What're you looking at? he said, shooting her a venomous look.

"I'm tired of being in my room and wanted something to drink." She took a swig from the can of fizzy water.

"Well, that might actually be true. Somebody told this Nguyen guy that I wanted Paige's job and didn't get it. Nguyen implied maybe I knocked her off so I was next in line. That came from you, didn't it? It's the way you think."

"Armando, I didn't even know you applied for the job. I didn't know you were in San Diego. You may be surprised to learn that I haven't been thinking about you at all."

"Um hmm. Well, who besides you knew about those bogus sexual harassment charges against me in Tucson?" *Who indeed? Margaret did. She and Armando were both on the board when that happened.*

"Maybe the police are checking us all out, Armando. Don't flatter yourself. It wasn't me." *Being the executive director has given me the guts to say things I never would have before.*

"Enjoy your soda, Missy."

"I will, Mister." *He's still doing that "Missy" stuff. Ridiculous.*

Lila must have been called to come in for her four o'clock appointment. She waved at Bea on the way in, and said, "Let's go into town early. Make a reservation and we can check out the coast over there."

"Done," Bea said. She went up the winding staircase and googled seafood restaurants, finding one downtown that sounded wonderful, and didn't take reservations, which she'd never get on a Saturday night at this late date, anyway. Salad with fresh crab. She was going to enjoy this trip, no matter what.

Then she figured that if the cops could do background checks, she and Google could, too.

Armando first. Nothing about those sexual harassment charges, which she (and Margaret) knew were the reason he didn't get tenure at the University of Arizona. There was a web site associated with his name... Encelia Biological, which was, "specializing in biological survey work in desert and coastal environments." This was clever; Encelia was brittlebush, one of those plants that had both desert and coastal versions. Armando had paid someone well for beautiful botanical illustrations of desert plants. "Artwork by Melissa McDowell." He cited work on two environmental impact statements in the California desert, and teaching a class on plant identification through the university's non-credit branch open to the general public.

He'd been in San Diego two years.

She didn't find much about Hank. He was on the La Jolla Gardens Board, of course, and the Coast Country Club Board, and he and a well-coiffed wife in a slinky low-cut red gown showed up in a couple of gala photos, where he was listed in the caption as a "prominent businessman."

Max Danes was on the Country Club board, too...

these people didn't seem to move too far outside their circles; her own board members were a little more diversified. Max was also on the opera board, where his profession was listed as "investor." Nothing more than that… don't call us, we'll call you. He was praised for his charitable contributions to the opera—a platinum donor. There he was, smiling with a wife about five decades his junior. She had the requisite flowing blonde locks and perfect body, well displayed in a royal purple designer gown. He looked awfully dapper with his longish white hair, tuxedo with a red cummerbund, and what looked like an ivory-topped cane. He also seemed to be on the board of a biotech company and a couple of dietary supplement companies. He probably made his money as a venture capitalist.

She sighed and looked up her own board member. Margaret Rhodes showed up in some Tucson charities, including the symphony, where she'd met the Gardens' founder, Liz Shandley. Before Liz met her untimely death four years ago, she had recommended Margaret for the board. She was described as the widow of Charles Rhodes, a builder in Tucson and La Jolla, California. Interesting.

Bea felt odd googling Lila, but she did and found an article about her getting shot. Thank God it hadn't been serious. That was part of the misadventures of three years ago. The shooter had never been found. But that couldn't possibly have anything to do with Paige's fall. It had to do with Lila's strident gun control op-eds. At least that's what the police had concluded.

Things had been so blessedly normal since then. No murders.

Bea realized she didn't know Camila's last name. How horrible! She knew everybody else's and she didn't know the last name of the pre-law student who was serving them meals. Bea sat staring into space, chastising herself. She sighed and googled Gertrude MacKenzie. There was no lack of stories about Gert and Mac's possible involvement in the illegal Native American artifacts trade, although they were never charged. There wasn't anything about those assault-and-battery charges, but that was so long ago. And obviously, the police had better access to those kinds of records.

She didn't really think she'd gotten anywhere with all of this. Lila knocked on her door, and said, "Let's go! I'll call a cab."

They shivered in the driveway, waiting for the taxi. The fog, which had slipped away for a few hours, was creeping back, softening the contours of the stone fountain, and creating swirls of mist from the falling water. It was quite beautiful, if you let yourself forget about water issues.

"It seems possible disagreements over water conservation have been roiling the board, but surely that wouldn't be a reason for Paige to jump off a cliff," Bea said.

"Good Lord, I hope not," Lila responded. They dropped the topic as the cab pulled up... who knew any driver's connections to anyone they might discuss? The car took them down a eucalyptus-studded hill. Below, they could see a pier jutting into the water. The driver followed their gaze. "Yeah, that's the Scripps Pier. You know, that oceanography place? They lower boats off it. You wouldn't believe how many people take sunset pictures underneath it. Perfect framing, then the waves breaking behind. Great surfing right there."

"Oh, are you a surfer?"

"Every minute I can. When I'm not driving or studying. I'm a student at UCSD."

"I guess there was a death on that stretch of beach right below where you picked us up." Bea might as well find out about the word on the street.

"Yeah. I heard it was ugly. You know the woman? I mean, she fell from that botanical garden, right?" he asked, turning to look at them. Bea clutched the door handle as he barely missed an oncoming car. There was little room to maneuver in these narrow, clogged streets, full now of families coming back from the beach, toting sun umbrellas and water wings.

"I didn't really know her," Bea said, and that was the truth.

She and Lila continued their conversation over delicious bowls of cioppino. The place they'd chosen was place a couple of blocks from the ocean, with a simple menu and a long display case full of local seafood. They pulled steaming chunks of fish from an herb-filled, rich tomato broth. Then they split a huge Dungeness crab salad and a plate of the local sea bass. Despite the prices, they had to share a long table with several other diners.

"This is why I wanted to come to San Diego," Lila said.

"Yep."

After they paid the hefty bill... made higher by a glass of dry French rosé apiece, and then another to share... they walked down to the shore, which was rocky here. The cliffs were just a few feet above the beach, unlike the ones by the Gardens, and there were a few small stretches of sand populated by honking sea lions. And people. Lots of people everywhere, ambling along the sidewalk above the cliffs and beaches. There may have been locals, but Bea heard French, Italian, Chinese, and some Slavic languages she could never begin to identify. They walked far enough to see a small beach roped off and covered with sleeping sea mammals, which a sign identified as seals. By the time their taxi arrived, they were thoroughly convinced that Paige had had a primo job living in this place, no matter how weird her board was.

Gert met them the minute they came through the door.

"That asshole Armando's in the ER," she announced.

"WHAT? He didn't fall off a cliff, did he?" Bea asked.

"Sort of. Guess he decided to go hang gliding this afternoon. It was on TV. His accident. You been noticing those guys flying around the cliffs north of here?"

"Yeah, I was watching them when we first arrived. I could see them out my bedroom window. He fell out of the hang glider?" Bea asked.

"Nearly did. There was probably something wrong with his safety harness. They said so on TV. Don't know why. He held on. Guess it's good he did all that weightlifting. You know, those bulging biceps."

"Is he all right?"

"Nope. Guess he's pretty bruised and has a couple of broken bones. That's what the reporter said. Armando hit the cliffs. But he's alive. And he's talking to the cops, I'll bet. And you'd better believe they're thinking about connections between these two things. Unless they were both accidents," Gert said with a cynical laugh.

"Armando has always been good at infuriating people," Bea said, with a grimace. All the fun had gone out of their expedition to town. Bea really needed to talk to Frank. She and Lila parted with a silent hug in the hall between their rooms.

Frank wasn't in the field; he was at some park service facility served by a cell tower, thank God.

"Hey, Bea. I miss you. She felt her toes uncurl just at the sound of his voice. "I'm done here and I'm hoping to see you at home tomorrow night. Think you'll be able to get there? If not, I could come to San Diego."

"Oh, Frank, surely they'll let us leave tomorrow like we were planning to. I wish you could come now, but you need to get home. Dad's not doing well. We can't ask my parents to do more than they committed to." She paused for a moment. "And there are unfortunate new developments."

"Now what?

"Armando got hurt in a hang-gliding accident. We

don't know anything except that maybe he had a loose harness."

"Why? Did he know what he was doing? Did he get checked by someone before he went out?"

"I remember his bragging about some hang-gliding exploits when he was on our board. I think he has experience."

"Well, the police should be able to determine pretty easily if the harness was tampered with. What else has been happening? How did your interview with the cops go?"

"It was pretty uneventful. But Armando was furious after his interview because they found out he had wanted Paige's job. Maybe they thought he would off her to get it now? And Gert was livid because they found she has some old assault-and-battery charges. She implied they were accusatory, but I'd take that with a grain of salt. And I had a talk with Camila and she is suing Paige's parents for treating *her* parents like dogs, although they were lifelong, loyal servants. Let's see… well, there are some motives right there. I have a lot more to find out."

"I'll bet you do. So, Bea, I'm doubting the accident theory of Paige's fall. What do you think about… I mean, you said she wanted to talk to you urgently… maybe she jumped?"

"Well, I told you she wanted to have a heart-to-heart with me... and I suspect it was related to 'challenging' issues related to her board. I mean to find out what those were. But it seems unlikely they got so *challenging* that she jumped off the cliff a few hours after she said she wanted to talk to me about them."

"Well, unless somebody talked to her about something excruciatingly challenging in the interim."

"Or unless somebody was worried about her confiding in me."

"I don't like that. That means you could be in danger."

"It's an unlikely possibility, Frank," she said to calm him down, but the rise in her voice betrayed her.

"Well, Lord only knows how Armando fits in. He was probably sticking his nose into something that he thought would benefit him."

"Things keep circling back to the La Jolla Gardens board. It does seem that at least Hank disagrees about whether they should display native plants, and there seem to be divisions about water conservation in general."

"It has to be about more than that."

"I think it's time I talked to Margaret. She knows these people."

"Well, that will give you something to work on. I know you can't just enjoy the ocean."

"I keep trying to do that, but *challenges* keep getting in the way."

"I love you. Be careful."

"I love you so much. Give the kids and Mom and Dad hugs for me and tell them I'll be there SOON."

It was too late to call her parents; they liked to go to bed early. She turned on her computer to check her email.

Her mother had written a couple of hours earlier to say that she'd had to pick Andy up from school the day before because he had a knife in his lunchbox. She was glad Bea had given her number for emergencies on Friday. Emma hadn't brought it up when Andy had called about the "sissy" stuff, because she didn't want to complicate his call. "It was a butter knife I gave him to cut his kiwi with. But don't worry. He's fine, other than being mortified. We're all fine. Just take care of yourself out there in the wilds of California. Your father thinks the butter knife thing is a grand joke. It's good to see him laugh."

That was a more concerning statement than the overzealousness of the school in the Andy incident.

There was also a message from Camila. Bea wasn't sure if she should open it before she went to bed. She was right. “I need to tell you something that may have a bearing on what happened to Paige. Come to the kitchen in the morning and we can set up a time.”

CHAPTER NINE

Bea's brain had been buzzing all night long. She knew she'd had several bouts of light sleep, but by sunrise, it was time to find some coffee. She put on the sweatpants and jacket she'd brought for beach walks or working out... she sure didn't need the conference clothes she'd brought for Sunday... and headed for the kitchen. Camila had preceded her, and good, strong coffee was ready. There was real half and half. Camila was sitting in a chair at the butcher block island in the middle of the kitchen, checking her phone. It rang.

"It's my lawyer," she said. "I'll call him back. There's plenty of time before I have to prepare breakfast."

"It's about your lawsuit against the Pearsons?"

Camila ignored the question.

"Come on, let's go have a cup of coffee in the garden. No one can interrupt us there," Bea said, zipping up her jacket. Camila nodded and threw on the sweatshirt hanging on the back of her chair She wasn't in uniform on Sunday morning. *That really would be over the top.*

Bea hadn't counted on Ace's nosiness. Well, maybe that wasn't fair. It was his job. It wasn't yet 7AM, so he was still on duty.

"What are you two up to?" he asked, taking that chart Bea had seen the morning before out of his shirt pocket.

"Just enjoying a morning cup of coffee before the day gets crazy again," Bea said, with what she hoped was a pleasing smile. Then she made a point of leading Camila toward the aviary, where the squawks of the awakening birds would protect their conversation from Ace or any other inquisitor.

They sat next to each other on a bench near a very loud cuckoo unlike any that Bea had ever seen; no doubt it was from Borneo or Panama or some other tropical place. Bea turned to face Camila.

"Great coffee." She waited.

"Well, ok, here it is. I don't really want to tell Detective Nguyen this. I think I'm definitely a suspect, so he won't trust me about it. Like I said..."

"The butler did it."

"Yeah. Well, I still don't think this is enough to make Paige jump off a cliff, but I can tell you that Hank Archer has spent the night here at least once." Bea caught her breath but managed not to react too strongly. Or so she hoped.

Camila gave her a bemused smile and continued, "I came over to meet with Paige one morning around eight, about another cooking job. That racist Ace almost didn't let me in, but I told him Paige and I had an appointment. So I opened the door and there they were, all rumpled and cuddled up together on the living room couch, almost naked. Hank jumped up and about bit my head off. 'WHAT do you think you're doing here?'" Her voice drowned out the bird calls for a moment.

"I said Paige and I'd arranged to meet, but I'd come back another time, and she said it was ok, but of course it wasn't, and I left right away. Hank was staring at my back; I could feel it. When Paige and I *did* meet a few days later, she said it'd been a mistake, and their 'personal relationship' was over. She seemed pretty broken up about it. How broken up, I don't know. He's very married. Every time I've catered a party in La Jolla, his glamorous wife Melanie is there, hanging on his arm."

Bea thought for a moment. "Well, do you think Hank would push her off the cliff so she wouldn't tell his wife?"

"Honestly, I don't know him well. I don't know how far he'd go." She gave a quick eyeroll.

"But you clearly don't like him."

"No. I don't. He's said some pretty nasty things about our lawsuit."

"Like?"

"Like it's better 'they' are in Mexico where they belong. After years of my parents serving him at the Pearsons' parties."

"Camila, I'm sorry. So… what about Margaret? Did she treat you that way? I find that hard to believe. But she's been acting odd ever since we got here."

Camila looked away. "I know she's your board member, and you liked her enough to invite her to this event." Bea had to strain to hear this comment over some very loud squawks.

"You didn't answer my question."

"No. She didn't say awful things about my parents." Bea looked at her for more information, but nothing more was going to be said. Camila was giving the gravel aviary path a good, hard look.

Well, it could be worse.

"Thanks for telling me this, Camila. I suppose we'd better see if some others are up."

"Well, I guess there's one more thing to add."

"Go ahead." *Now what?*

"Melanie Archer was very rude to me the last time I served her at a party. Ruder than most people. She said something about me 'staying in my lane.' At the time, I thought she meant the lawsuit. But it was right after I discovered Hank and Paige together. Could she have had it in for Paige? I don't think it was serious between Hank and Paige. Frankly, it seems more likely that Melanie would try to do something to me, a known rabble-rouser. But this is just more information for you."

"Gee, thanks."

Camila didn't look to be amused by the sarcasm. "Really, Camila, thanks for trusting me enough to say all this."

"Maybe it can help get me cleared. Judging by that detective's questions, the Pearsons have definitely been trashing me."

"I'm so sorry."

As they headed towards the house, Ace looked over at them, and pulled out his playground monitor sheet again.

"Isn't he off duty yet?" Bea asked.

Camila looked at her watch. "Should have left ten minutes ago," she said. "He doesn't ever work more than he has to. Maybe he's playing amateur detective like you."

Bea looked to see if there was anything other than friendly ribbing in that comment. She couldn't tell; Camila's face was impassive. Bea changed the subject. "I'm wondering if Armando's accident fits into all this," she said. "Any ideas?"

Camila stopped and gave her a hard look. "I don't know." She picked up the pace and entered the house well ahead of Bea in a way that belied their roles as confidantes.

She's not saying something. Or somethings. The only person I really trust around here is Lila.

It was time for breakfast, and Camila wasn't smiling as she brought out the yogurt, fruit, and granola, and filled their dainty flower-patterned coffee cups. Lila and Gert were already at the table; everybody else lived off campus. Except Armando, who was in a hospital somewhere. Bea had never liked him, but she wouldn't wish a major accident like that on anyone. Camila had reverted to the persona of a servant. She wasn't looking at anyone and responded to Lila's question about how she'd slept with a curt "fine." Bea just couldn't read her.

The front door banged open and Hank blew into their uneasy gathering. He held a rolled-up newspaper that he banged on the back of the couch. "Have any of you seen

THIS?"

Gert said, "Well, we don't know what 'this' is, but if it's the local paper, no, not a one of us hailed a cab to go find one this morning."

"Right," Hank said, looking at the people he'd been yelling at. "Sorry. None of you have subscriptions."

Bea forestalled another retort from Gert by asking, "There's a story about Paige?"

"Damn right, there is, and it's a travesty. They quoted some old boyfriend who said she had "bad judgment" about people, and implied somebody could have killed her out of retribution. Then somebody on our board... and I think I know who... said that Armando had applied for her job and was better qualified. That guy couldn't hold a candle to her!" The last statement was delivered with a loud whack, as the rolled-up paper hit a wooden end table.

"Why would your board member say that?" Bea asked.

"Hell if I know. No respect for the dead. She deserved better than this!" He threw the paper on the table and sat down. "Camila!"

"Yes?" she said as she came out of the kitchen. There was a hint of mockery in that "yes."

"I need coffee."

"I'll have to brew a new pot. It'll be ten minutes."

Lila and Bea caught each other's eyes. There had been plenty of coffee in the pot after Camila had filled their cups a few minutes ago.

Bea looked at Hank, stretching his legs out under the table, getting ready to opine. How could Paige have been romantically involved with him? She thought back to college. Paige had dated high-status guys, including the man she married. Bea had known one of the early boyfriends. He'd said something like, "All the professors here give Asian students a leg up." Bea had avoided him after that.

Hank's sigh brought her back. "Well, ladies, here's what I know. The officers are over at the Pearsons' right now, giving Paige's shattered parents the extensive interview they deserve. I'm sure they have a lot they want to tell him. The cops are going to be talking to others who live in San Diego at their own houses... Max and Margaret, I guess. I don't know, maybe he'll interview that board member who blathered to the newspaper reporter. Anyway, he wanted me to tell you that you may be getting texts for second interviews, so do what you want to do, but you need to be able to be back here in an hour to an hour and a half after you get a text."

"Well that shoots down seeing the San Diego Zoo," Lila said. "Although I looked up the admission charge, and I wouldn't go anyway. All that talk we had about admissions... it's nearly fifty bucks!"

"For the love of Pete, are we gonna be able to go home tonight? I planned to camp in Borrego Springs tonight. Then back to Copperton tomorrow." Gert shook her head in disgust.

"I have a 6PM flight that I really need to make. I'm a parent, and this is the busiest time of year at my garden," Bea said.

"I'm just the messenger," Hank protested. "Where's my coffee, anyway?"

"You're so gol' darn impatient. It hasn't been ten minutes yet," Gert told him.

Hank's phone dinged. He picked it up, read a text, and yelled, "That was the security agency. Now Ace has up and quit! Nice of him to let me know. Now we've got no security guard at night! I'd better get on the phone with this damned agency." He stomped out. Camila came through the swinging door with the coffee pot just as he was out of sight.

"Refills?" she asked.

They all nodded. These pretty little cups didn't hold

much coffee.

Lila was looking at something on her phone. "The aquarium's pretty close. Anybody want to go there with me when it opens?"

"Might as well. I'm not up for another stinky beach walk," Gert said.

"Um… I was thinking I might pay Margaret a visit," Bea said.

"Really? Don't you want to take a break?" Lila's look was reproving.

"Well, no. She *is* my board member. I feel like I should check in with her in all this mess."

"Suit yourself." Lila said this with raised brows. The gray eyes lingered on Bea's face. Bea set her jaw. Lila sighed and turned away from her. "I'll see if I can line up a taxi to the aquarium, Gert."

"Find out if we can walk."

CHAPTER TEN

Bea called Margaret and asked if she could come over that morning. "I've been expecting you to say that. We have some things we should discuss."

"Good. Margaret, I'm thinking Detective Nguyen might call me back in, and I have lots of questions. Maybe after we talk, I'll have some ideas to mention to him."

"Why would he want to talk with you again, Bea?"

"Well, it's pretty well-known I couldn't stand Armando."

"By that logic, I merit a second interview, too. Come on over, Bea. I have all kinds of teas. You can walk here. It's just a few blocks away. No ocean view from here, I'm afraid. It's one of the smaller, older homes. 425 Breeze Way."

Bea walked four blocks inland from La Jolla Gardens. Some of the houses were older one-story properties on this street, and some had clearly been remodeled or built up to showcase huge ocean-facing windows. All hid their back yards with hedges or elaborate iron fence work. Bea glimpsed a tennis court in one yard. Margaret's street was lined with Bea had come to recognize as surfer vehicles, parking in strictly time-limited spaces.

Bea rang the doorbell to a home with an immaculate rose garden in front. Margaret opened the door herself, and gave Bea a hug, saying, "Bea, dear, thank you for coming," an intimate gesture that was a bit of a surprise. Inside, the ceilings were lower and the rooms smaller than those at La Jolla Gardens, but it was not a small house. Family portraits supervised the living room. "That's my husband Charles," Margaret said, as Bea looked at a painting of a jowly man with thin, pressed lips which belied a twinkle in his eye. Or maybe the twinkle belied the pressed lips.

"Tea?" Margaret had about eight kinds of tea bags on a little tray with two tiny floral cups. *I'm okay with cups like this in the afternoon, when I'm not needing my caffeine infusion.* Bea pulled out a ginger tea bag. "This would be perfect."

"That's the first perfect thing that's happened this weekend. Bea, there's something you need to understand about this whole situation with Paige and her parents and Camila."

"There does seem to be some tension between you and Camila."

"She's suing some very old friends and being quite slanderous."

"She told me about the suit."

"Oh she did, did she? And did she mention she's suing me as well?"

Bea almost dropped her cup. "No, she didn't mention that."

"We spent a whole year out here several years back. The Pearsons were in Europe, so we became Camila's parents' full-time employers then. They still lived in the house on the Pearson property and took care of it." Margaret gulped her tea. "You know, Bea, I'm hardly surprised that Camila didn't mention it. She wants you on her side. I can see it."

"That may be true. But what does that have to do with what happened to Paige?"

"Well, Paige took Camila's part, for a while, but the Pearsons talked sense into their daughter. She's always been close to them. She did a great job in the family business, and then when she wanted to apply for this executive director job, her father supported her in doing that, even though he'd set his heart on her taking over from him when he retires. He told me he thought she still might come around. That it might have been a passing fancy."

"Wait a minute, Margaret, back up. Are you implying that Camila would kill Paige because she switched her position on the lawsuit?"

"It's a possibility. She probably already felt betrayed when they stopped spending so much time together, you know, when Camila went to public school and Paige went to the academy."

"That would be an awfully longstanding grudge. But yeah, there are a whole lot of possibilities." *Including that you're trying to manipulate me. You asked to come this weekend. You weren't my first choice, but I thought it would give us a chance to get to know each other better. Is that happening?* "Margaret, I have several questions."

Margaret took a long sip of tea. Quietly. Then she lifted her eyes. "Yes?"

"I can see why there's tension between you and Camila... But you seemed to be cold to Paige, as well."

"Yes. Well. That's perceptive of you. I felt it was a bit of an affront that she hired Camila and I had to be faced with someone suing me. That's a minor beef, Bea. Of course I'm horrified about what happened to Paige."

"Okay. That's it?"

Margaret nodded, looking down as she did so. "It seems petty now."

Bea shrugged and went on. "Now, what is going on with this La Jolla Gardens Board? You know them, right?"

"Some of them. Well, all but one." She gave a little laugh.

Bea raised an eyebrow.

"First of all, you need to know about the Edisons, John and Chrissy, who donated the Gardens to the public. They were lovely people. Their parents were some of the first in La Jolla. I think they came in the 1920s. He came from money in New York, then went into banking here. Anyway, John grew up here, went to Wall Street, but came back. He knew Hank Archer well. Arthur Blakely—you know, he's on the board, too, I think he's the secretary, but they pay somebody else to be the recording secretary—Arthur and my husband Charles played tennis doubles against John Edison and Hank. They were a golf foursome, too. Max—you know, Max Danes, he came to the Gardens for dinner on Friday night—he was also a good friend of theirs. They all did business together, too, usually successfully. Well, they had a loss or two, but Charles always said that's the mark of a good businessman. Successful men aren't overly cautious, he always said." She shook her head as if to ward off a thought and gave a false little laugh. *What about successful women? Not part of Margaret's picture.*

But she had no chance to ask, because Margaret continued, "As I think you know, I lost my Charles ten years ago now. John and Chrissy died in a car crash in Monaco three years ago. Their will said they wanted their home to become a public garden, and they wanted Hank and Arthur on the initial board. Plus someone else."

"Is that someone else the person you don't know?"

"Oh, I know her, all right." Margaret gave a bit of a snort. A ladylike snort. "You see, the Edisons were avid singers. They loved choral music. Their choir director was this young Indian woman—you know, Indian from India—whom they kind of adopted as a daughter, almost. She was at all their parties. I think they even went on a cruise with her."

"You don't like her?"

"Samira is an excellent musician. In addition to singing, she plays viola with a chamber music group. And I have no reason to think she didn't genuinely like the Edisons."

It sure doesn't sound like you think that.

"But?"

"But she caused dissension on the board, Bea. We both know about board tension. Our friend Armando provided us with plenty of that, didn't he."

Bea was not going to go there. "So what did... Samira... do to cause tension?"

"She felt they needed someone with more landscape or plant knowledge than any of them had. She also thought they should balance out the white men on the board with another woman. So she came up with Maria Alvarez, who's on the faculty at UCSD in Landscape Architecture. *She's* the one I don't know. But Hank tells me there's never a dull moment at board meetings. And he didn't mean it in a good way."

"Is it this native plant business? I get it that some of the board favors replacing some of the original plantings with natives. And water conservation, is that part of the disagreements?"

"Yes, it's been women versus men on those issues, so Hank came up with Max to change the balance on the board. The way he thought it should be. I guess Samira voted with the guys to put Max on the board, probably because she knew he was an old friend of John and Chrissy's and she wanted to honor their wishes. Maybe she felt guilty about bringing Maria on, since so much discord ensued. I don't know."

"Interesting."

"Oh, honey, it gets more interesting." Margaret fingered her ever-present pearls and Bea wondered whether she slept in them. "So Maria decided they needed to balance out another white man, I guess, plus she thought they needed another plant person. So she's the one who suggested Armando. He applied for Paige's job and didn't get it, and Maria heard about that, and checked him out. The board hasn't voted on Armando yet. That's why Max came to hear him talk. I let Hank, Arthur and Max know what I thought of him when we had to deal with his uncouth behavior on *our* board."

"If Armando got on the board, it would be a three-to-three vote on these issues we've talked about, huh. And maybe other issues as well."

"No doubt." This time her snort was not so ladylike.

"So, Margaret, I have a question. Are the men also the only officers on this board?"

"I believe that Samira's the VP. And I think Hank would like to hand off one of his jobs—treasurer—to Max when he comes on. I guess it's not 'best nonprofit practice' or something like that for someone to have both jobs, president and treasurer. Of course, nobody wanted either job, so Hank stepped in, but he needs to drop one."

"Actually, I think it may be illegal in California, but I don't know for sure." Bea took a sip of tea and set her cup down, leveling her gaze. "This is all very interesting, Margaret, but do you think it has anything to do with what happened to Paige? Or Armando?"

"Well, it *did* occur to me that those women might prefer Armando as executive director to Paige. But I've known Samira for a long time. John and Chrissy adored her. I have difficulty believing she'd get involved in foul play."

"But you think Maria might."

"As I said, I don't know her. And... as to who would try to hurt Armando, well, I imagine that could be most anyone, don't you? Some woman he offended, or some man whose honor he'd besmirched."

Bea let that one drop, although Margaret certainly had a point. But Bea had to mention something else. "So if I'm hearing you right, you think either Camila or Maria had good motives to murder Paige." She tried to keep her tone from registering disapproval, but apparently she failed, because Margaret retorted,

"No, I am not a racist, dear girl. Just a realist."

There was something else she might as well ask Margaret, as long as she had her ear. "Margaret, did Hank and Paige get along? The executive director/board president partnership is so important."

Margaret set her teacup down with a clatter. "Good heavens, you wouldn't be suspecting Hank of foul play! He's one of our finest citizens. And he's very pleased with Paige in her role as director. I'm sure he's fond of her. His wife doesn't like her. She told me so. But Melanie is probably just jealous of a much younger woman spending so much time with him. She's like that, you know. The jealous type. But Hank adores his wife." Margaret shrugged her shoulders at the foolishness of Melanie's sentiment.

Margaret is a fountain of information. But it seems likely that Melanie may have had reason for jealousy.

"Well Margaret, it's been interesting hearing your take. Thank you for talking to me about it." *I don't want to get on **this** board member's enemies list if I can help it.* "Margaret, have you told Detective Nguyen all this?"

"I have very little confidence in Mr. Nin. I thought I'd tell you, instead. You did a good job of solving that last murder, at Shandley Gardens."

"He seems quite competent to me. I'd rather you talked to him directly."

Margaret sniffed.

Bea reflected, as she often did, on her luck of being born blonde, blue-eyed, and very white. And thus, apparently, more competent than a policeman, in Margaret's eyes.

It was also interesting that both of the women she'd just talked to wanted her to bring their concerns to Nguyen. For entirely different reasons.

CHAPTER ELEVEN

Bea walked into the lobby of the Gardens just in time to receive a text from Nguyen, who wanted her to come in for another interview. She texted back that she'd be there right away.

I'm becoming quite familiar with this mansion. She laughed out loud for a moment, thinking about how dear Angus, struggling with brides and rude employees back in Tucson, would rib her about hobnobbing with tycoons.

She knocked on the office door. "Come in, Ms. Rivers." Nguyen's voice was flat and professional "Take a seat, please."

As she sank into a cushy green leather armchair facing the desk, she looked around at the now familiar room and felt a wave of sadness. Paige was dead, for no good reason. What on earth had she wanted to tell Bea?

It turned out that the reason Detective Nguyen had called her in wasn't her antipathy towards Armando. He was thinking about Paige, too, and wanted to probe Bea's relationship with her. "We have eliminated an accident as the cause of death. The cliffs were stable where she fell. There is no evidence of rockfall anywhere nearby. It is unlikely that she stood too near the edge, since she installed the sign warning people back. We have not, however, ruled out suicide. Paige's parents said that she seemed depressed of late. She had started to see a psychiatrist. She wanted to talk to you about something that was concerning her a great deal. Have you had any further thoughts about what that might have been?" Bea's eyes went to his hand, which was poised with a mechanical pencil over a pad of yellow legal paper filled with notes. When she hesitated, he drummed a couple of times with the pencil.

"I really don't know. I've been asking myself about this, but I just don't know. I'm sorry." She stopped, and he drummed again, once, as though he knew there was more coming. "I did find out about some conflict on her board, although it's really hard for me to see it as important enough to make anyone throw themselves off a cliff, or to commit murder."

"Go on."

She told Nguyen what Margaret had told her.

"She didn't see fit to enlighten me with these theories."

"No." He probably suspected the reason why.

"So have you done any more sleuthing, Ms. Rivers? I gather you're an old hand at this."

Bea blushed. "Well, I did find out something about Hank Archer. At least, according to Camila."

She told him about their possible affair, and that Camila believed it was over. And that Hank's wife was rude to Camila, possibly because she'd caught her husband in a compromising position.

"I see. Anything else, Ms. Marple?"

Bea swallowed her impatience and didn't retort, but she waited several beats before replying. She hoped her pause would give *him* pause about making that sort of jab.

"Well, no doubt you know this..."

"Very possibly not, I'd say."

"Well, you must know about Ace Karlsson's white supremacy rants online? And rages against 'elites'?"

"Yes, Ms. Rivers, we do." His shoulders relaxed a bit when he said this. His voice was a little gentler when he said, "Anything else?"

"No."

"Well, do let me know if anyone else confides their

theories in you. You are planning on leaving this afternoon?"

"I have a 6PM flight."

"At this point, that should be fine. We'll be in touch."

Hmm. Does he think I'm just a patsy who'll get the cops on the wrong track? I'm not going to believe that. These pieces fit together somehow. Now I really want to figure this out. It doesn't seem like Nguyen is buying Camila or Margaret's ideas, but he hasn't really told me anything. I owe Paige my best effort in getting justice for her. If she jumped, who made her feel she had to do it? If she was pushed, who could have been that inhumane?

Bea went down to the living room to keep an eye on the door, and on who was going in and out of the office. Gert had left her room and was going in now. She looked at Bea and called out, "More fun and games!" She started to knock on the door, but it opened.

Bea found a lovely little pad of paper embossed with the La Jolla Gardens name, which featured one of the South African king proteas. She found a pencil on the coffee table and began to make out a list.

It began with Hank. She could see why he might have tried to kill Armando. Did he hire somebody to be a fake employee at the hang-gliding port, pretending to make sure Armando was safe? He might have thought Armando had pushed Paige over the edge so that he could get her job. Hank certainly didn't want Armando as executive director. But as for murdering Paige... he'd shown emotion about her death, and the defamation in the newspaper. Was he just acting? Was he afraid Paige would tell his wife about his liaison? Hank had left the group early the night that Paige fell and hadn't been on Ace's list of night strollers. She remembered that that list had contained Paige, Armando, Gert, and Camila. Those who'd stayed up drinking the first night... and had been serving the drinkers. But couldn't Hank have come in by a back route?

He lived in the neighborhood...

For that matter, couldn't anyone come by a back route, if there were one? Surely the detectives were investigating non-La Jolla Gardens people who might have had it in for Paige. Without their resources, she'd keep thinking about the people she knew about.

Now what about Melanie Archer? She made a new column for her. Bea had never met her, and she'd just seen her photograph in the society pages online when she'd first done those Google searches about people at the weekend meeting. It seemed like at least a week had passed since then. Melanie had reason to be jealous of Paige. Maybe she'd hired someone to push her? But Armando? Why would she want to hurt him? Surely he wasn't having an affair with the wife of the president of the board he wanted to serve on. Well, it *was* Armando, after all. Every attractive woman presented an opportunity.

She made a third column for Camila. She seemed way too smart to be pushing Paige off a cliff because she favored her parents' side of the lawsuit. Camila would want to stay within the law, partly because she knew she was vulnerable. But Camila had concealed the fact that she was suing Margaret. Bea couldn't and shouldn't entirely trust her. Nor, clearly, did Camila trust Bea.

Ace had said Camila was walking around the grounds "in the middle of the night." *Is my natural sympathy for Camila affecting my judgment?*

And then there was Margaret. She was certainly trying to use Bea to pin the blame on Camila and the only other Latina, Maria, in this mix. But could she possibly have been angry enough about the lawsuit to have Paige killed? Margaret surely did not push her off the cliff. For one thing, she wasn't physically strong enough. She did hate Armando. But Margaret really didn't seem like the murdering type. Words were her weapon.

She should also consider the possibility that Armando's accident was not related to Paige's fall. If that were the case, then Armando might have tried to kill Paige to get her job. And had an actual accident at the Gliderport.

And of course there was Gert, who apparently had assaulted someone (more than once, she'd said) in her youth. But Bea had such a hard time seeing Gert wanting to kill Paige. Armando was a more likely target for Gert, but he'd probably inspired more animosity from other people—he was good at that—than Gert bore him.

She was working on an "Ace" column. It began with "hates elites." But somebody was ringing the doorbell. Insistently. Bea counted five rings. So much for her list.

She peered through the peephole.

It was a woman in her mid-to-late forties, disheveled, red-eyed, weepy. Clutching what looked like a letter. Bea opened the door a crack.

"This is where the cops are? About that girl that fell off the cliff?" the woman asked, after blowing her nose into a used tissue.

Bea was regretting opening the door, until the woman said. "I need to know. I'm Ace's mother. Ace Karlsson. He's my boy. A security guard. I think he's in trouble because of her. That woman who fell down to the beach."

"Detective Nguyen is talking to someone else right now, but I'm sure he'll be out soon. Why don't you come in, Mrs. Karlsson."

She stepped just inside the door, which Bea closed and locked.

"Please sit down." The woman sank into a chair in the front hallway, just beside the door. "May I get you a glass of water?"

Mrs. Karlson stifled a sob. "Yes." A huge sniff. "Thanks."

In the kitchen, Camila was slicing fresh tomatoes. "Lunch. It's the last meal I'm contracted for this weekend," she said. Bea thought she heard "Thank God," but she couldn't be sure. She nodded and filled the water glass. She went back through the swinging doors, through the dining room, and out to the hallway, where she gave it to Mrs. Karlsson, who drained it in a couple of gulps.

Silence. Mrs. Karlsson was twisting her hands. She reread the letter, which looked to be a short scrawl on a much-abused piece of typing paper.

There was no way Bea could continue with her own scribblings. She was just about to say she'd knock on the office door to alert Nguyen, annoyed as he'd undoubtedly be by that interruption, when Mrs. Karlsson said, "He'd better hurry up. My boy told me not to worry, but I'm worrying plenty."

She pulled the overgrown fading reddish bangs from her eyes with a quick, rough swipe. "See, he says he had to go to Mexico, but not to worry, he's doing the right thing for America, even if it means leaving his country to save it. I'm not supposed to try to find him and he doesn't have a phone now. What am I supposed to think? I know he didn't like working here. Is somebody here after him? Did they chase him out of the country? Maybe the person who killed that girl?" She blew her nose. Bea went to the bathroom and brought her a fresh box of tissues.

Fortunately, Gert showed up just then. The office would be free. "That guy Nguyen sure holds his cards close, don't he," Gert said.

Bea gave Mrs. Karlsson her hand and pulled her up. "Come on. I'll take you to the room where the officers are interviewing people. I know they'll want to talk to you."

Gert was silent, for once, but she gave Bea a flabbergasted frown.

Bea had to hold Mrs. Karlsson's arm on the way down the hall. She kept sniffling.

Bea knocked on the office door. "Who is it?" Nguyen sounded annoyed.

"Bea Rivers. With Ace Karlsson's mother. She needs to talk to you."

"I see." He opened the door, gave Bea a hard look, noticing her grip on the other woman's arm. "Come in, Mrs. Karlsson." He said nothing to Bea, who started back to the living room.

Camila rang a lunch bell. They hadn't needed one for the other meals, but everybody was so discombobulated today, it was probably necessary. Lila's door opened. "Cattle call for lunch, I guess," Gert called out. Bea hurriedly retrieved her notes on the living room table and jammed them into her pocket.

"I'm thinking it's just the three of us, right? Plus Camila. Maybe we can get her to sit with us," Lila said.

The front door opened, and Margaret was escorted in by Hank. And another woman. So much for their intimate gathering. Why did Hank always insist on bringing outside guests for meals?

"Guess the gang's all here. You'd think they'd want to stay home, for Pete's sake," was Gert's next comment. It was loud enough for everyone to hear, of course.

"Well, this was to be our final meal, and Margaret and I thought it best to be together. And I thought it would be nice for you all to meet my wife, Melanie. We want to send you home on a positive note!" Hank said.

Is that really why he's here? Well, I can't say I regret meeting Melanie and checking her out.

"Yes, I asked Hank to bring me here to meet you all." She turned her head towards him, her fluffy ponytail swishing as she did so, and gave him a frank look that asserted it was her idea to come, not his. He nodded.

The ponytail swished back, and Melanie directed her large brown eyes on Bea. "I'm glad to meet you, Bea. I've heard quite a bit about you. Sorry for coming in tennis clothes. I just got off the court." Melanie extended a hand to Bea. She wasn't sweaty. Her hand was smooth, long and elegant. She didn't look like she ever broke a sweat. "And you must be Lila." She extended her hand again. Her right hand had a sapphire ring. Bea couldn't get a good look at her left hand, but the ring on it was undoubtedly impressive.

"And I'm Gert," Gert broke in. "Hope our little group is up to your standards."

"Is there any news?" Margaret asked, possibly because she was anxious to know, or because she wanted to forestall more interaction between Melanie and Gert.

"Well..." Bea began, and then stopped. "Ace Karlsson's mother's in there with them right now. She's pretty upset."

Camila emerged from the kitchen with a platter heaped with fresh tomatoes, basil and thick white mozzarella cheese. The gazes that had been fixed on Bea were pleasantly diverted.

"Beautiful!" Bea commented.

"The veggies are all from the garden here." Hank was back in expansive host mode.

Margaret was clearly about to ask a question, when Camila emerged again with a basket of fresh bread and a plate of something... "Smoked yellowtail from our local seafood supplier," Hank informed them.

When Camila disappeared once again, Margaret asked, "What was Ace's mother upset about?"

"I don't know," Bea replied. This was mostly true, and it was certainly true that she didn't want to repeat what she'd heard. Her earlier insight had been right on target: she surely didn't know whom to trust.

The conversation turned to the deliciousness of the ripe, sweet, dribble-down-your-chin tomatoes.

"What were the best tomatoes you've ever eaten?" Bea asked, in a conversational tone that was better suited to lighter times. Hank and Margaret agreed that the tomatoes were extraordinary in Italy, "especially around

Naples," Hank added.

"No dear," Melanie said, with a noticeable coolness, "we both agreed that they were better in Tuscany."

Hank was conciliatory. "You're right, Mel."

Gert said she doubted they could compete with her family's Texas tomatoes. Bea said she hadn't had a better tomato than the one on her plate.

"Hear, hear," Lila said.

Then the office door opened, and Mrs. Karlsson emerged from down the hall. Her hair, a sort of orangey blonde that seemed to be a step in the redhead aging process, had escaped a barrette in the back. Her eyes were puffy, and she was using what looked like a fresh tissue, no doubt provided by Nguyen, to wipe her eyes. When she saw the five of them staring at her, she hurried towards the front door. They watched in silence as she tried to tug it open, and Bea, Hank, and Lila pushed back their chairs and headed towards her to help, but she succeeded in escaping the house. She banged the door shut.

Those standing resumed their seats. Margaret said, "I wonder if that Officer Nin is going to tell us what is going on."

On cue, the office door opened. Nguyen's already thin lips were tightly pressed together. He walked briskly into the dining room and stood before them. "Is Camila Gomez here?"

"In the kitchen," Bea said. "I'll get her."

Bea was only halfway out of her chair when Camila swished through the doors and stood against a wall, arms crossed. Detective Nguyen looked at her as he said, "I just wanted all of you who are in this house to hear this."

Camila loosened her arms, but they were still crossed.

She's had a lot of experience having to protect herself.

Detective Nguyen aimed his gaze at each of them in turn before he said, "I regret to say that Ace Karlsson has disappeared. We have been unable to find him, and now we have information that he may have left the country for Mexico." He stopped, surveyed them all, and resumed talking in the same measured tone. "I would like to ask those of you who do not live in San Diego to stay another night. Please do not follow Mr. Karlsson's example. I cannot legally force you to stay, but it would be best for all of us if you do."

Lila and Bea caught each other's eyes.

Maybe if I stay, I can figure something out that will help the case. I'd like to do that for Paige. Frank will be home now. I'll call him and see what he thinks. I got the flight on Southwest Airlines miles, so I can change it without penalty.

"I was planning on staying in Bea's guest room in Tucson tonight, before I drive back to Copperton. It's kind of up to Bea. And if I can change tickets without an upcharge," Lila said.

"Well, hell, I was planning on camping in the desert tonight. I've had about enough of La Jolla, I can tell you that. You already have my cell phone and email and everything, probably more than I know about. I'm leavin'!" Gert said.

"Very well. We will stay in touch with you. Bea and Lila, you will let me know ASAP? And the rest of you live here," Nguyen said, looking at Margaret.

"Yes, I was planning to stay for the rest of the week at my home here anyway," Margaret said.

"Of course, Hank and I will help you out in any way we can. I'm sure you'll solve this all soon." Melanie said. Hank was watching her intently, but she was focused on the detective. She smiled at him. *That's a practiced smile guaranteed to make men feel good about themselves. I wonder if it will work on Nguyen.*

"Right. Good." He scanned them all again. "Now then, Camila, I believe we have an appointment in half an hour."

"Yeah."

And that was it. He executed a nearly military turn,

and went back to the office, as they watched.

"Mexico!" Margaret said, as though it was as far away as Tasmania.

"Sounds like he was fleeing the law to me," Gert mused.

Maybe. But what was that about doing the right thing for America? I'm not going to mention that to anybody but Frank.

"Well, this puts a damper on our goodbye luncheon. At least I assume it's goodbye," Hank said.

Melanie was scrutinizing Bea.

"I'm not sure what we'll do." Bea looked to Lila for confirmation. Lila shrugged. "But thank you for the hospitality, Hank."

"Such as it's been." He grimaced.

"Even if we stay, we probably won't see the rest of you again," Bea said.

Hank pumped her hand, then Lila's then Gert's. "I hope to meet you all in better circumstances."

Melanie's scrutinizing look was now directed at her husband.

"Come by before you go, Gert," Bea said. Then she went into the kitchen with Lila and said goodbye to Camila, who would no doubt be leaving the place the moment her kitchen clean-up was finished. Camila nodded at them both and said, "Have a safe trip." Her phone rang. "I really do need to talk to my lawyer," she said as if they were trying to prevent her from doing so, instead of coming to say a friendly goodbye. There was no recognition of the intense conversation she and Bea had shared.

Bea returned to the dining room and waved goodbye to Hank, Melanie and Margaret, shouting, "See you in Tucson!" at her board member. Before heading upstairs, she watched them get into their cars. Melanie was shaking her head at Hank. She got into the passenger side of the Jaguar with a loud bang of the door.

Bea turned away from them all and walked up the ridiculous staircase to her luxurious quarters, stopping to watch the cars leave the driveway from the landing. She went into her room and settled in an armchair facing the sea.

CHAPTER TWELVE

When she called, Frank answered after one ring, and told her everything was fine at home, that the kids missed her, but he got it that she wasn't ready to leave the mystery unsolved. "That would be completely out of character, Bea. Go ahead and stay. I don't have to be at work until Tuesday. It'll be a leisurely Monday morning. Do what you need to do."

They both laughed. Getting the kids off to school ran from hurried to flat-out frantic.

"I'll try to leave here in the morning. I can answer emails in the airport. And I can work from home in the afternoon. Angus won't be enthralled with being in charge another day, but he's got a nice vacation coming up. You and I can talk some things over after the kids get to bed."

"Sounds good."

"How is my dad?"

Frank hesitated a moment. "Your mom's taking him in for some tests tomorrow. He's been having abdominal pain. We'll see."

"Not bad enough pains to go to the E.R.?"

"He certainly doesn't think so. They're treating themselves to a couple of nights at the Arizona Inn. Much needed after the rigors of childcare at our house."

"I feel guilty."

"Don't. Meanwhile, what's your current theory about what's going on in La Jolla?"

"Well, for starters, Ace fled to Mexico. Which looks awfully suspicious."

"Slow down. He did what?"

"The police say he's gone to Mexico. And his mother showed up here, totally freaked out, and said he'd written her that he was "doing what's best for the country." His blog said he hated 'elites' Would he have thought Paige was "elite" and knocked her off?"

"Seems horribly possible. This cop *is* going to let you come home tomorrow, right?"

"I'm coming home tomorrow no matter what. Lila, too. She'll need to spend the night with us before she drives home. He can't keep us here, he said. At least unless he arrests us."

"Well, I won't worry about you. Unless somebody else gets killed. Then things would be getting a little too close to *And Then There Were None.*"

"Nguyen already called me Miss Marple."

"Promise me you'll be careful, beloved sleuth. Here's Andy."

"Mom, you'll be here for my concert on Wednesday, right?"

"You bet, Andy."

"Jessie, quit grabbing the phone!"

"She's my mom, too! Momma, Frank says I can't have popsicles every night, but Grandma lets me!"

"If Grandma's in charge, she sets the rules. Frank's in charge now."

"Ohhh, no fair!"

Frank's voice in the background said, "Why don't you guys get ready for Alice's birthday party. You'd better hurry." She heard running feet, then, "I'm back. I love you."

"Thanks for doing birthday party duty."

"That was always part of the deal. You weren't supposed to be back until after dinner anyway. But I'd better go."

"You're the best. See you tomorrow and I love you, too."

She turned to the window and watched the breakers. God, she was lucky. Six years ago, she'd been so lonely, wondering if having children meant you had to give up any joy except the wonder your babies provided. Then Pat had left her, and child rearing got harder, especially when he cancelled family days and nights. She was working full-time at Shandley Gardens when she'd met Frank. She kept him at arm's length for a while. Her kids certainly didn't need another betrayal, and neither did she. Slowly, she realized Frank meant what he said. And then there'd been a telltale night when she'd jumped out of bed four times because Jessie was feverish and crying. Frank smiled at her dedication. Pat would have been pissed he'd be off his game at work in the morning. That was when she knew she could marry Frank.

She broke her gaze from the surfer-dotted breakers, and the kayaks beyond them. Her eyes went to her computer. *Might as well see if there's any news of our calamities here.* She typed in "Armando Ramos." Maybe there'd be an article about his mysterious accident.

And there was. It had been determined that an "unknown person" had checked his harness before he launched. Police had not determined a motive for what might have been incompetence but could also be foul play. Armando described this person as a female, white or Latina, medium build, dark brown hair in a ponytail, mid-twenties, wearing a San Diego Chargers baseball cap and sweatshirt. The Gliderport, the launching port for hang gliders, avowed absolutely no knowledge of her. There was a quote from Ramos, and a photo.

"This imposter, an attractive young woman, actually undid a buckle, then zipped me back in, and I didn't know there was a problem until it was too late. I'm lucky to be alive. I plan to sue the Gliderport."

He looked pretty terrible in the photo, with a leg cast, crutches, a sling, a neck brace, and some very ugly facial bruises. He was standing outside a hospital flanked by Hank Archer, who was not mentioned in the story.

Hank gets around. And I wonder if Armando was more than willing to let a young woman check him. The woman wasn't Ace unless he was wearing a wig. And I don't think Armando would have seen him in any guise as an attractive woman. Camila has black hair, and she's certainly attractive. Armando thought so the first night… but he would have recognized her. Unless she had some kind of disguise. I'm sure Detective Nguyen will check her alibi.

Ok, back to the computer. What happens if I google Paige?

There was nothing new here, except a memorial service would be held the next month. In lieu of flowers, donations were to be made to La Jolla Gardens. Her parents were devastated, and asked readers to respect their privacy.

And Ace?

Here she struck paydirt. There was late-breaking article in an English-language newspaper published in Tijuana. A man had found a body in a ditch outside a Tijuana slum. He said the victim had been shot. There was no money in his wallet, just a driver's license with the name "Ace, last name beginning with a K." Apparently, a local reporter had discovered this much and had called the police with the approximate location given by the person who'd found the body. That person had vanished just after talking to the reporter. The Tijuana newspaper had not tied Ace in with La Jolla Gardens, but it was only a matter of time before someone in the media did.

Oh, my God, his poor mother.

Assuming it really is Ace.

It seems likely somebody wanted him found. Otherwise, why not bury him, and why leave his driver's license on him?

Was the guy who told the reporter involved in the

killing?

What was it that Frank had said about *And Then There Were None*?

She needed to think carefully. She came out of her room and found Lila hugging Gert goodbye in the hallway.

"Be careful, Gert," Bea said, and gave her a half-hug, which was all Gert would suffer from her.

"It's safer out there in the desert with the coyotes and bobcats, I can tell you," Gert said. "It's humans that's the problem."

Gert went out the front door, shaking her head. Lila turned to Bea and said, "Ted Nguyen and the other cop tore out of here like bats out of hell. Hey, Bea, you are *pale.* Things getting to you?"

"Yes, they are. Ace might be dead. That poor kid. In Tijuana."

"Come into my room. Let's talk this through."

Bea followed gratefully. Lila sat on the bed, and gestured Bea towards her armchair. Bea sank into pillowy softness on all sides.

She focused on a beautiful photograph of a sunset over the ocean. The lightness of the pink clouds eased some of the weight she'd been carrying in her shoulders. She took a few deep breaths and told Lila what she'd read.

"Hold on, friend. Let me google Ace and see if there's anything new."

Lila googled Ace but there were no news updates. She closed her laptop and turned to Bea. "Do you think that Nguyen is going to let us know what's just come down?"

Just as she asked, they got simultaneous texts. Detective Nguyen told them that Hank Archer had hired another security guard for La Jolla Gardens, from a different firm, who'd be arriving at 7:00. Meanwhile, the neighborhood guards who drove around—both day and night shift—were going to concentrate on watching the Gardens. "We have an unconfirmed allegation that Ace

Karlsson was shot in Tijuana. When this is confirmed, we will let you know. Please inform me if you are staying the night."

"Do we really want to do this?" Lila asked.

Bea wasn't at all sure they wanted to stay, but it was worth finding out if they could get on a flight the next day at a reasonable hour, and if Lila could do so without penalty. A quick call revealed that there were no barriers to changing their flight.

Lila sighed. "Now we have to make a decision."

"We're probably as safe here as anywhere with these security guards around. I say let's do it."

Lila nodded slowly, as her eyes penetrated Bea's.

"Let's go down and talk to the security guy in the car; I have a couple of questions I want to ask him. And I'd like to look through Paige's room; I saw the cops in there earlier, but there's no crime scene tape or anything. And frankly, I'd like to look at the office, although they may have locked it up," Bea said.

"Okay." Lila nodded more vigorously. "We need to stick together."

They changed their tickets, and texted Ted Nguyen that they'd be at the house until 10:00 the next morning.

"The fog's creeping in off the ocean again," Bea said, as she reached for her jacket. They went down the stairway. It was a relief not to have any onlookers in the empty house, as they descended. The thick fog had slid up the cliffs and was spilling onto the driveway, heading for the road. They made for the street, as well, and began looking for the little car with "SafeT Security Services" on the door. They passed numerous boxwood hedges, their dark green leaves barely visible, and several stone walls and high gates, some with royal-looking logos. No one was walking in the immediate neighborhood, except for a Latin American woman wheeling a small white child in a stroller... maybe she'd come off the bus Bea had seen the morning before. *Thirty-plus years ago, that could have been Camila's mother and Paige.* There was also and a Spandex-clad young woman with two poodles.

Bea and Lila circled back towards the road to the beach. For three blocks on either side, beat-up vans and compact cars squeezed into tight parking spaces. Barefoot muscled men and women approached cars with wetsuits unzipped to the waist.

"Didn't we see that the water was fifty-eight degrees when we went out yesterday?" Lila asked.

"What brave souls."

A well-coiffed executive towel-changed out of a three-piece suit. After they had walked by, Bea turned around to see the result; in about a minute flat, the guy had gone from work suit to wetsuit. He was now carefully hanging the work suit inside his BMW. Three beat-up cars with surfboards drove up; it was rush hour on the roads and the waves. But where was the SafeT security guard?

They turned around again, heading back towards La Jolla Gardens, and the SafeT car was parked in front. They walked to the driver's side. A young, athletic-looking Asian woman rolled down the window and told them that the Gardens was closed for the day. The skin not covered by her uniform was decorated in tattoos.

"Oh, we definitely know it's closed," Bea said.

The woman squinted at them suspiciously. Her name tag said "Allie Chung."

"We're the two people staying the night here. Thank you for looking out for us," Bea said.

The woman's squint relaxed.

"Would it be okay if we asked you a couple of questions?"

"I guess."

"Do you always work the day shift?"

"No. It depends."

"Were you by any chance working the night that Paige

Pearson fell off the cliff?"

"Wait a minute. I don't think I should be answering your questions. The cops already talked to me. They know what they need to know."

"So, she was a friend of mine. It sounds like you were there that night..."

She didn't deny it.

"I just wanted to know if anybody drove to the Gardens, or walked to the Gardens, after 11:00 or so."

"I told the cops, and I'll tell you, too. When those three luxury cars pulled out that night, nobody came back before I got off shift at 7:00. I did NOT fall asleep: I was watching carefully."

"But couldn't somebody have slipped into the house while you were patrolling the rest of the neighborhood?"

"Normally I'd say yes, but Paige... Ms. Pearson... asked me to drive down the driveway far enough to 'check on things' several times a night for a few nights. She's been pretty decent to me, unlike *some* people around here, so I kind of based myself out of here. Kind of like I'm doing right now. I even checked on some of the people whose cars I've seen in the Gardens this weekend. Some live in this neighborhood. No lights, no movement in their houses. You know, just in case."

"Wow, thanks for taking such good care of us. Were the people you checked on 'decent' to you, or maybe not?" Bea said.

Allie Chung's reasonably friendly demeanor shut down. She stared at them. "What did you say your names were?"

They pulled business cards out of their wallets. Chung looked at them and her expression softened. She stuck her hand out the window to shake their hands and introduced herself. "So you're garden directors like her. Well, I hope somebody figures out what happened to her. Everybody around here's already upset enough about having a garden and home open to the public right in the middle of this residential neighborhood, and now they aren't too happy with a murder. At least that's the rumor, is that it was a murder. Thank God they're not blaming me." She broke her gaze a minute, turning towards the steering wheel. Then she nodded her head, as if she'd made a decision, and said, "They also say she might have thrown herself off that cliff. I don't believe that theory, myself. You don't want to cross people around here. I'm guessing she did. And that's all I'm saying. I said as much to the detective." She stopped Bea's question before it formed. "And no, I'm not about to mention any names. So, you take care of yourselves. How long are you staying there?"

"Til ten o'clock tomorrow morning."

"Okay. I'm working some extra hours tonight. Until midnight. And take my advice, don't nose around where you're not wanted. Always a good policy." She put her foot on the accelerator and moved off.

"Thanks!" Lila called to the car's bumper.

Just then, A BMW pulled up to them with a Spandex-clad blonde at the wheel. "I saw you talking to our security guard. I hope there's nothing wrong in the neighborhood?"

"Oh, no. We were just chatting," Bea said. There was no point in sparking rumors.

"That's good. She's the best one we've had in that job for a long time. Eagle eyes, that one. She even found my lost cat. There's been way too much going on around here lately. Looks like you were trying to pay that garden a visit." She gestured with her head towards the La Jolla Gardens sign. "It's closed. Hope it stays that way. Better not to have a public garden in our neighborhood." She nodded goodbye and zoomed off before they could come up with a response.

Bea pulled her jacket tighter. "She's probably one of the people who doesn't want public events at the garden.

Remember Hank's problem statement our first night?"

"That seems ages ago. But yes, it looks like neighborhood antagonism may be real. I wonder if it has anything to do with all the foul play?"

"Not sure. And why would Paige ask Allie Chung to keep a watch on the driveway?"

"Well, it could be just good hostessing."

"Or something else. And I hope Detective Nguyen gets more out of her thoughts about the neighbors than she's telling us. Come on, let's go look at Paige's room."

They turned towards the house as Lila said, "Bea, I'm not convinced we should get ourselves any more mired in this situation than we already are. But okay, I'll look at her room. Let's leave it at that."

The front door was locked, which was novel, in their experience at the Gardens. Maybe Camila had locked it when she left. Bea pulled out the key that Paige had given them when they arrived.

They walked to Paige's room on the second floor, just down from their own. Bea knocked, just in case the police had returned, unbeknownst to them. No answer. She turned the doorknob, remembering that Paige's room looked different from the rest of the house. She hadn't paid much attention to the décor when she'd checked for Paige when she was missing at breakfast on Saturday morning... She did remember a cacophony of colors, unlike the calm pastels and seascapes like those in Lila and her rooms.

The images arrested her this time. Paintings of tropical birds filled the walls, along with rainforest scenes replete with sloths and tapirs. There were colorful desert scenes, too; photographs of swaths of poppies and lupines, and one of bright yellow prickly pear cactus blooms. Bea felt momentarily homesick. A band of coatimundi climbed red canyon walls. The bedspread was covered in scarlet macaws.

"Looks like Paige loved to travel… either in reality or in her dreams. Dramatic, colorful travel. The bed is neatly made. I remember you told us that when you checked on her, Lila said.

"Yeah, no peaceful ocean sunset pictures here like there are in our bedrooms. She had no strong sense of place for the California coast, it seems. Look, there is *one* of some southern California plants. I think that's California lilac in bloom, over on that wall."

"Yes, I think so, too. Interesting that it's the smallest, least conspicuous work of art here. It's not the room of someone who celebrates their home."

"Maybe she really wanted to get even farther from Daddy's business and her upbringing than she had, so far." Bea sighed." I wish I'd insisted on finding out what was bothering her Friday night. Maybe I could have helped."

"Now, Bea, don't take *that* on." They studied the room again, turning to look at the artwork Paige had chosen. "Well, we're not likely to find any computers, or cell phones, or journals, or letters," Bea said.

"Nope. The cops will have those. Whose photographs are on her desk?"

"Looks like her parents."

They stood a moment and contemplated the older couple in formal dress, arms entwined, blowing out the candles on a cake.

"Kind of sad that Paige doesn't have any other pictures," Bea said, thinking of the pictures of her parents, Frank and the kids, and a couple of old friends on her own desk.

"Also sad that she won't live to be the age her mother is in that photo. Her mom looks happy."

"Let's check out her books." There was a small wall bookshelf above the desk. Bea began to pull out the titles. "*Responsibilities of Nonprofit Boards, Difficult Boards, The Role of the Executive Director, The Challenges of Nonprofit*

Leadership. Wow, she was really working on being a good director. Look, there are also several yoga and meditation books. Trying to de-stress."

"That's the top shelf. What's on the bottom?"

"Here's what she probably actually enjoyed reading." Bea pulled out a paperback novel and turned it over to read the back. "Hmmm. This one's about a New York heiress who was transformed by meditating in India."

Lila pulled out another. "This one's a memoir. A birder left his secure job as a stockbroker to spend a year birding around the world."

"I'd like to borrow this one, although that's probably not too wise at this point. A family with two small kids sails a small boat from California to Australia."

Lila pulled out another novel. "This was written in the 19th century. Jungle exploration."

"Here's one about the early days of the Desert Laboratory in Tucson. You know, work there began in 1903. That was quite an adventure, trying to learn about desert plants, which were like something out of Lewis Carroll. Boojum trees were even named after a creature in a Lewis Carroll poem."

"I hope she got to do some adventuring. I suspect she felt like throwing over the lessons in *The Challenges of Nonprofit Leadership* for something a little more fun."

"Who wouldn't?" Bea asked, but even as she said it, she knew that, despite some issues on her board, and some difficult personalities—Margaret's came to mind—she wasn't longing for a different life. "Margaret really made it sound like Paige left the family business for the excitement of this nonprofit job. But neither is as exciting as birding around the world or throwing everything over to live in an ashram in India. You're right, Lila. Part of her was straining to break the bonds that held her."

Bea sighed and continued, "Maybe Paige really was unhappy enough to kill herself. Maybe she was clinically depressed, and the break-up with Hank and the fights on the board were enough to make her want to escape her world altogether, not just through books and paintings."

"Maybe."

"How about if we take another beach walk. When we get back, we can call our husbands again. I'd like to walk, and I'd like to walk when it's full daylight out, if you know what I mean."

"You bet I know what you mean."

"We can tell that security guard in the car when we plan to be back."

"Excellent plan."

They went out the lobby door, past the formal fountain, which was still enshrouded in fog.

"It's interesting that almost all of San Diego's water originates in the Sierra Nevadas and the Rockies. Very little of it's local. Armando was right about that."

"Because of the engineering systems of earlier decades. Dams. Pumps. But it's hard to out-technologize climate change."

"Yep."

They walked in companionable silence for a bit, past the high hedges, until they caught sight of Allie Chung just short of the now-familiar surfer parking. They waved for her to stop.

"You guys okay?"

"Yeah, we're just going to head down the road to the beach. We'll just be gone an hour or so. Thought we should let you know."

"Good plan. I'll keep an eye out."

"Thanks," they chorused.

"She definitely makes me feel more secure, whether or not that's warranted," Lila said.

"I'll take it." Bea looked at her and they laughed, a little overlong, over their newfound concern over taking a simple walk.

They headed down the road to the beach. The tide was lower than it had been before, but they once again kept away from the cliffs, keeping to the water's edge.

Bea found a sand dollar. They stopped to watch a couple of brown pelicans swooping down through the fog to fish something out of the sea. Bea waded out to her knees in the frigid water and spotted a school of small, silvery fishes that she vowed to identify when she got back to her computer. She emerged from the ocean shivering but calmed.

"I'm starting to get as grumpy as Gert. The sooner I get back to the high desert, the better. But you fit here, Bea."

"Probably not socially, at least in this neighborhood. But I do love the ocean."

They walked by the cliff below the Gardens and stared up the three hundred feet to the top for a bit. They could barely make out what looked like palm trees on top. Huge rocks had fallen below the Gardens... not recently, they'd been told.

"We can avoid this particular danger. Easier than some others around the Garden. Let's get away from these cliffs," Bea said, as she led the way back to the water's edge.

"I don't know, Bea, if you wanted to kill yourself, wouldn't that be a tough way to go? Poison or overdosing on pills would be easier than that long, scary fall and awful impact. And she had a psychiatrist. She had access to pills."

"But it seems she did have an attraction to drama. Given her room. I keep coming back to foul play. Armando standing next to Hank in that photograph taken after his accident. Maybe Armando knew he had support and thought he could finally be executive director here. Since he didn't succeed in his plan to replace *me* when I was just acting director at Shandley."

"What's your theory about what happened to Armando, then?"

"As my board member Margaret said, he's sure to have plenty of enemies."

"True enough. And how is poor Ace tied in? Or isn't he?"

"It still seems possible that he thought he was doing something good for America by getting rid of an elite. Maybe he found out something about Paige that made him think she was evil, in his book. Or maybe somebody bribed Ace to do the deed and then he ran."

"Armando?"

"God, I don't know. Uh-oh, we're getting near that nude beach area. I don't really want to see those guys striking poses for us again. Let's turn around."

They headed back down the beach. Bea shivered a bit, from her soaking or maybe from contemplating the murderous intent of several people she knew. They turned up the road that led to the top of the hill. About halfway up, Bea started to pause at the overlook where they'd lingered on their last walk up this road. She could see the white of breaking waves framed by cliffs on both sides of the road. A voice coming from her right felt familiar. She turned to face two well-dressed middle-aged men on the far side of the overlook.

One was Hank Archer; it was definitely his emphatic voice, the voice that had dramatized his points by banging on the dining room table with a knife just a couple of days ago. Lila must have had the same realization, because she, too, had turned away from the view, and was looking at the men.

Bea could hear them far better than she could see them. Not only was it foggy, but they were facing away from her, towards the ocean, as they talked.

"He's the wrong type for us, Arthur, absolutely the wrong type. We can't get this board off on the wrong foot."

Bea wasn't surprised that Hank was lobbying against Armando... surely that's who he was discussing.

Arthur, isn't that the name of one of the guys in the tennis foursome? The two others, John Edison, the Garden's original owner, and Charles Rhodes, Margaret's husband, are dead. Arthur is on the La Jolla Gardens board.

Arthur had turned his head to look at them. He probably thought Hank was being a bit indiscreet. Hank turned, too, paled a moment, and snapped into his hail-fellow-well-met mode.

"Bea! Lila! What a surprise! Isn't this a lovely walk? But I thought you might have opted to head out of our little mess by now."

"We've decided to stay until morning," Bea said, and wondered if she should have mentioned this to a possible killer.

"Well! Enjoy the rest of your stay and please come back in calmer times!" Hank's tone continued to be jolly.

"We hope to," Lila said coolly.

"We hope there's a swift resolution to the question of what happened to Paige," Bea said.

Arthur had been regarding them closely through a pair of wire-rimmed spectacles. "I gather you two are part of the group that met at the Gardens this weekend?" he asked.

"Yes. Poor Paige." Bea shook her head. "And Armando, too. And Ace, apparently."

Arthur's forehead wrinkled. "Who is Ace?"

"You know, our security guard. He skipped work and there's an unconfirmed rumor he was found dead in Tijuana," Hank said, with a shrug of his shoulders. It seemed that's Ace's disappearance wasn't worth taking any time to discuss.

"Good Lord, Hank! This is far too much negative publicity for the Gardens!"

"Arthur's in public relations," Hank said, which Bea

thought was a poor excuse for Arthur's callous attitude towards Ace's fate. Hank's wasn't any better.

"We'd better be going," Bea said. "I do hope to return to visit the Gardens in better times."

"See that you do," said their jovial host. Bea and Lila trudged up the steep hill as a few surfers raced down. Bea turned around to see the two men shoulder-to-shoulder in hushed and undoubtedly non-jovial conversation.

Bea was preoccupied and unaware of her surroundings when Lila elbowed her. "Look!"

She was pointing to a path that ran along the top of the cliffs towards La Jolla Gardens.

Lila said, "It's a neighborhood path!"

"Hank or Melanie Archer could have used it to get to the cliff edge at the Gardens."

"Almost anybody could have."

"But maybe all these people employ personal security guards."

"But they know the Archers."

"I wonder where they live."

Just then Allie drove by and gave them a wave. "All's well?"

"Sure," Bea said.

CHAPTER THIRTEEN

"OKAY, LET'S CHECK OUT THE office," Bea said as they went through the front door. "I'm going to get some gloves. There must be some under the kitchen sink."

"Wow, what are you contemplating?" Lila asked.

"I'd like to get into that file cabinet. And see whatever else there is to see… that is, if the police have left anything there."

"Oh, Bea. Okay, I'll come with you. As long as you don't break any locks. Let's hope Ted Nguyen is dealing with stuff in Mexico and doesn't make a surprise visit while we're in the office."

They walked over to the desk. It was absolutely clear. Not even a notepad, and certainly no computer, or calendar, or to-do lists.

"Such a stunning room," Lila murmured.

"Let's find the key to the file cabinet. Friday night she put it under that fossil."

Bea lifted the ammonite, but there was no key. It wasn't under the music box, or in any other obvious place in the room.

She tried the file cabinet door, hoping the police had left it open. No such luck. Maybe they hadn't opened it, and that trove of files was still in there? Unlikely. "No doubt the cops removed the key along with everything else of consequence. Including her files," Lila said.

"I don't really want to break into the file cabinet. At least not right now."

"Agreed," Lila said.

"I need to call Frank. Let's call home and regroup. We're going to have to think about dinner. I don't know about you, but I'm all for take-out, at this point. I feel safer with that SafeT security guard patrolling out there. I like her. And I guess there's a new one coming to patrol the grounds, too."

"Let's meet up in an hour and order dinner. It's already 5:30."

Just then their phones buzzed. The text was from Nguyen. "Mrs. Karlsson has made a positive identification in the morgue of her son Ace."

Bea let out a long sigh. "If I hadn't met him, I'd think it was the cartels. But I can't believe Ace was involved with them. He said what he was doing was good for America. And what could this possibly have to do with Paige and Armando?"

"Let's sit in the jacuzzis in those luxurious bathrooms... when will we have one of these again... and call our husbands, Bea."

Bea nodded her head and headed to her room. First, she locked the door and tested it. Then she kicked off her shoes, pulled the curtains, stripped down, and turned on the warm water. She brought her phone over and, unwilling to wait, got in as the tub was filling. When it was half full, she turned on the jets and sank down. The soreness in her shoulders, her marker of responsibility, began to ease. She sat up and picked up the phone. Frank answered on the second ring.

"Hey, Bea. I'm hoping things have calmed down a bit."

"Not exactly. Ace got murdered in Tijuana. We don't know much about it, but it's hard not to wonder about connections..."

"Bea! It sounds like maybe this is turning into some dark gangland thing... please, please be careful. Now I wish you'd made a decision not to stay!"

"I'm leaving tomorrow morning. For sure. We've got

security guards here and on the street."

Frank exhaled loudly.

"I know. I just want to be home."

"Now that their grandparents are gone and they're headed to school in the morning, the novelty of the week-end has worn off, and the kids want *you.*" Bea felt immediate guilt. He read her feelings without her saying a word. "We're fine, Bea. Do what you think you should do."

"What do you think about me trying to break into Paige's file cabinet? Nguyen would probably figure out it was me and would charge me with interfering in an investigation. I have no idea how to do it anyhow."

"You can google it. There's probably a You Tube video. But I suggest that instead you get some great fish tacos or something and read a book. Something super diverting. You've got your Kindle there, don't you? Don't read a murder mystery. Then tomorrow get a cab and come home! I'll make up the couch for Lila."

"That's good advice, Frank. I know it is."

At six-thirty, she knocked on Lila's door, and found she'd gotten similar advice from her husband Eddy. They checked out places that had good tacos and a carry-out service and made their order. Then the doorbell rang.

"That's too fast for our delivery," Lila said." Let's check it out together." They went downstairs as the bell rang again.

Bea looked through the peephole. "It's two women. They *look* like normal people."

The door had a letter-slot sized opening with a sliding cover. Bea stood on her toes, slid it open, and asked, "May we ask who you are?"

"Certainly! You must be Paige's guests. I can understand why you'd be nervous. Crazy stuff happening! I'm Samira and this is Maria. We're on the La Jolla Gardens board and we're looking for Officer Nguyen." The woman speaking was about Bea's age with a South Asian accent.

She and the slightly older Latina looked like people she'd welcome inside, under ordinary circumstances.

Bea and Lila turned to face each other. Lila raised her eyebrows, and Bea shook her head.

"Officer Nguyen hasn't been here for some time," Bea said. She hoped that would take care of their interest, although she did have questions for them...

Allie Chung stepped up to the doorstep and turned to the women. "May I help you?"

"Hi," Bea said through the door. "These two women say they're on the La Jolla Gardens Board and they're looking for Officer Nguyen."

"He's not here, and these people aren't accepting visitors."

Maria grimaced, but Samira said, "Oh, we understand. He cancelled our interviews until tomorrow, and he hasn't answered our calls. We need to talk to him."

Bea was thinking she really should let them in and have a chat, but Allie said, "I'll let him know you're looking for him. He's asked me to check in after the new security guard for the property arrives."

"Thanks. Well, ladies, I hope we can meet in better times," Samira said. "And I hope your boards are more copasetic than ours." Maria gave a disgusted laugh at that remark. Bea watched them walk to a Tercel that was nearly as weathered as her own. *No luxury cars for those two.*

"Allie, thanks again for keeping an eye on things here. There should be a Door Food delivery here pretty soon, just so you know."

"This doesn't look like a delivery," Lila said, as a young man emerged empty-handed from a small red pick-up truck.

"He's got on a uniform. Different company from Ace. Hank said he was hiring from a different firm. This must be the new guy." Feeling ridiculous for hiding behind the door this long, Bea opened it and put out her hand to shake the new security guard's hand. "Bea Rivers."

"You're one of the two women I'm supposed to be watching out for tonight," he said. "I'm Chuck Fox." Chuck was older, far more muscular, and more assured than Ace, who'd had the air of a high school kid hoping for an invitation to the cool party on Saturday night. Fox pulled a business card out of his pocket.

Lila came out and introduced herself. Chuck wrote down his phone number on the back of the Stronghold Services card. "I don't have my own cards printed up yet. Text or call me if you have any concerns." He gave his number to Chung, too, who handed him her business card. She gave another to Bea, "for good measure." Bea tucked both cards into her jeans pocket.

Chuck said, "Mr. Archer wasn't happy with my predecessor. Guess he didn't do such a good job of keeping folks safe. That's not gonna happen."

"Glad to hear it, Chuck. Now that you're here, I'll go back to my rounds." Bea saw Allison punch a number into her phone as she walked off. Was she calling Ted Nguyen? Bea had an idea.

"If you don't mind, Chuck, I'll just send your photo to the detective conducting the investigation here. He wanted to know when you showed up to help out."

"No ma'am, I don't mind."

Bea pulled her phone out of her pocket and sent off the photo.

"Thanks. We're expecting a food delivery any moment now. We don't plan to leave the house for the rest of the night."

"Good idea, ma'am. Mr. Archer told me to alarm the house. If you really don't plan to go out, I'll set the alarm in an hour or so. Let me know if you change your mind and go out, even to look at the stars." He pointed to Bea's jeans pocket. She took out the card and had to twist her lips to keep from chortling at the Stronghold Services logo, a cartoonish medieval fortress surrounded by spear-carrying sentries. The gangplank was up.

"Okay, we'll definitely tell you if we want to go out, but it's unlikely. It's good to know we have so much protection."

Before she and Lila went back inside, the delivery van showed up. Chuck Fox watched while a young man who looked a lot more like Ace than he did gave them a huge plastic bag filled with Styrofoam taco containers. Fox waited while they tipped the delivery person, who drove off in the van.

Fox gave a curt nod. "I'll be checking things on the grounds. Don't forget to let me know if anything happens."

"Got it," Bea said. She turned to Lila. "Our husbands worry too much."

CHAPTER FOURTEEN

Bea and Lila loved their dinner. They each had three broiled fish tacos, but one was served with a mango cilantro slaw, another with a traditional tomato, onion, and chile salsa fresca, and a third with an avocado pineapple salsa. The blue corn tortillas were tender and earthy, and they'd ordered extra mango slaw. They found some Mexican beers in the fridge, and Bea felt like she'd come to a smooth, groomed trail after a long, rocky bushwhack with a number of near-falls.

They'd each opened a second bottle of Bohemia when Bea's phone rang. She pulled it out, hoping it was Detective Nguyen, back from Tijuana. She'd felt uneasy when Samira and Maria said they couldn't contact him.

But it was Margaret. Bea sighed and answered the call.

"Well, my dear, I hope you're in Tucson now, and well out of the mess here."

"No, actually, Lila and I are staying until tomorrow morning."

"Oh."

"Oh, what?"

"I do wish you'd made a different choice."

"What's done is done. We just had great tacos."

"Tacos schmacos, Bea. Since you're still here, I just feel… I just feel I need to tell you something."

"Please do."

"I don't know what happened to Paige, or Armando, or that young security guard, either. But I have lived a long time, and I know that there are a number of people who have money and power and can get what they want, and you, Bea, do not want to cross them. My dear Charles was close to many of these people. They believe they became wealthy because they are superior human beings who have earned more rights than others. Don't do any of your investigating here, like you did when things went awry in Tucson three years ago. You are dealing with a whole other level of power. Enjoy the house, sleep well, leave in the morning, and I'll see you in Tucson soon."

"Margaret, do you know something specific that I should hear?"

"That is not the point of this phone call, dear girl."

"Your point is just to give a general warning? It sure would help if you told me what or whom I need to watch out for."

"Be careful and you'll be fine."

Bea sighed. "Thank you, Margaret. See you in Tucson." They disconnected.

Bea stared at the phone as if it were a human.

"What?" Lila asked.

"She wants me to stay out of trouble. It's unanimous."

"Here's another vote. I'm gonna find a light movie on that big screen in my bedroom. Something stupidly funny. Want to join me?"

"Nope. I need to think. My mind's a whirlpool. There's something swirling in there that I can't quite pull out."

Lila gave her a long hug. "I'm done with La Jolla and all this." They took the dinner garbage into the kitchen and returned to the living room. Lila headed up the dramatic stairs, beer in hand. She waved before closing her bedroom door.

Bea wavered a little when she thought about pursuing things without the balm of her friend's kind gray eyes and careful listening. Then she swallowed and went back into the kitchen.

Everything was neat and put away, the counters had been scrubbed; the place looked like nothing had happened there in the past few days. Camila was done with her job and done with them, Bea suspected. She couldn't see how Camila would be involved with Armando's accident and Ace's death. Margaret had said that Paige's parents would implicate Camila in Paige's death because of the lawsuit. Were they the people Margaret was warning her about? But what about that woman with the San Diego Chargers gear at the Gliderport? Could that have been Camila? She could have had a good reason to hate Armando: what else was new with attractive women? But Ace? Why Ace? Well, Ace hated immigrants....

Bea didn't like where this logic was leading her. She felt sympathy for Camila's parents' story. How horrible to devote your lives to taking care of a family only to have them abandon you when cancer struck.

But she had to follow all possibilities.

Hank's actions were confusing. He'd shown what *seemed* to be real distress over Paige's death. He'd told the security guard to be extra vigilant for Lila and her own safety. But he didn't like Armando and didn't want him as the next La Jolla Gardens Director. And he thought Ace was beneath his concerns. But it was hard to imagine Hank hiring somebody to off Ace in Tijuana for a job poorly done. On the other hand, maybe she was just being naïve.

She went back to the living room, picked up her unfinished Bohemia, and considered their first night in La Jolla.

Paige had put a lot into the menus, and agenda, the details to promote conviviality. Who does this when they're considering suicide? She'd singled Bea out that night. They'd gone to her office, chuckled over banana slugs...

Bea sat up with a start, put her beer on the table, and went to get the kitchen gloves, again. She put on the gloves even before she opened the door. *Never too soon, at this point.*

Yes, she'd caught it only in the corner of her eye, but there was indeed a banana slug. It was a small ceramic piece, on a window ledge, not with all the beautiful Oaxacan animal carvings. She walked over to it and picked it up.

And yes, there was a key underneath it. She sucked in her breath.

It could fit some other lock. The cops probably have the only key to the filing cabinets.

But it turned smoothly in the lock. A tingling current ran through her right hand, up to her elbow. She pulled out the highest of the three drawers. There were just a few folders, falling in on each other. She pulled out the other two drawers, which were much the same. *Clearly, Nguyen took anything of any significance.* Of course they'd done their jobs properly.

She began to check the folder labels. They must have taken anything related to the board, or personnel, or money. What they'd left was gardening information. There was a file on pollination, one on cycads, one on California native plants, one on irrigation, one on pest control, one on winter color. Bea paged through them. It was all very straightforward.

And a bit of a letdown. She felt herself slumping in the chair, and then straightened up and looked into the pest control folder. What pests were they dealing with... termites in the tool shed, it had to be tented; castor oil granules for gophers, banana slugs... *This must be Paige's idea of a joke. Banana slugs live in the deep, wet green of the Pacific Northwest.*

She opened the file. There was just one pink sticky note inside, and it said, in neat cursive, "in the compost bin." Well, she did remember that some people had thrown slugs that were eating their veggies into their compost bins... in the redwood forests of Santa Cruz. But she couldn't imagine that they could survive in this land of ten inches of annual rainfall, even in a wet compost bin. It was exceedingly odd. She would check out the bin with her trusty headlamp. Years of camping had made packing it a habit.

Paige might have been signaling something to her. Bea *had* found a key under the banana slug after they'd talked about slugs and Santa Cruz. Or she might be over-thinking it that this was a personal message to her.

If Paige was actually worried about her safety and wanted to leave Bea a clue in the compost bin of all places... well then, Bea had to check out the bin. There was that security guard, Chuck Fox, out there, and this would be a test of whether he was on the ball or not. She'd come up with something if he asked what on earth she was doing.

Bea put on her fleece jacket and pulled her headlamp over her hair.

But Chuck Fox had probably set the alarm. She raced down the stairs, two at a time. There it was, blinking steadily by the front door. It was definitely on. Well, she'd tell him she wanted to take a look at the stars. He'd even suggested that. And this was the first night that the sky was partially clear.

She went back up to her room, found the card he'd given her on her desk, and made a call.

"Hi, this is Bea Rivers inside the house."

"Miss Rivers? Is everything ok?"

"Yes, thanks. You were right." *It's always good to lead with that to gain somebody's confidence.* "I'd like to look at the stars, since I'll be able to see a few tonight. And I'd like to smell the ocean since I'll be heading back to the desert tomorrow."

"Too bad for you that you have to go back to the desert."

No, it isn't. "I'm actually looking forward to seeing my family."

"Ok, I'll turn off the alarm. I'll wait for you by the back door in ten minutes or so."

Guess I'm going to have an escort.

She paced around the room and then went into the kitchen and found an apple; she could put the core in the compost bin. She also picked up the pair of gloves she'd been using, after making sure they were well washed and dried. She would toss these gloves tomorrow, even if it was reasonable to wear them to dig around in compost. She raced up to her room and put an earring in her pocket: she had a scheme. She rattled the back door but he wasn't there. *What's taking him so long?* She paced by the window and focused on the lights far out at sea. Were they fishermen?

Fox opened the door and said, "Come on out."

"Oh, hi, Chuck. What are those lights out there?"

"Oh, those are squid boats. Guess you don't have those in the desert, either." He smiled in what looked, at least in the dark, like commiseration. Bea felt irked, as she always did when people disparaged the desert. But she had more important things to worry about.

"It smells heavenly. So... this is kind of embarrassing..."

He looked at her sympathetically. *I'm getting good at sucking up to him. It's kind of revolting.*

"I do want to look at the stars, but I have another reason for coming out here now."

He raised an eyebrow.

"Well, I was helping to clean up breakfast this morning. putting stuff in the garbage and the compost, and one of my earrings must have fallen out." She pulled a little silver frog earring out of her pocket. "See? They look like this. My earring isn't anywhere in the kitchen or my room, and I checked right afterwards. It's happened before...

loose backing. My father gave the earrings to me, so I'd hate to lose one. I'm thinking went into that big compost container over there..." She motioned to the large plastic bin by the vegetable garden. I think it'd be near the top. I won't have to dig through, because nobody's been on duty since... we lost Paige... to turn the compost. I'll just check it out with my head lamp."

"Well, I guess that would be okay. Why don't I help you look?"

"It's really not necessary."

"What else do I have to do?" He grinned at her. Oh my God, I think he's flirting. *I should have said the earrings were a present from my husband, even if Dad really did give me my favorite frog earrings.*

"Well, if you think that's best." She didn't meet his gaze, which she could feel appraising her.

They walked over to the bin and Bea pulled on the gloves. "Kind of yucky to root around in here," she announced, as she started to pull off the top. Chuck intervened and lifted it off with a flourish. Bea began to claw through the compost and Chuck stepped back. She wasn't sure if he was giving her room to maneuver, or if he was repulsed by the smell.

There were clearly no huge bright yellow banana slugs. There was cantaloupe, and tomato, basil, and toast from recent meals. There was also a lot of older, moldier, stinkier stuff. She felt quite ridiculous, with this guy behind her shining his huge light into a wet, smelly mess. "I can't believe you're messing around in that disgusting pile of you-know-what," Chuck said.

But Bea had found something. "Oh, look! You're not supposed to put plastic in compost bins. I'll just remove this and take it inside and put it in the real garbage." She took something from the side of the bin.

"What's that?"

A piece of paper with a whole lot of numbers on it in-

side a clear plastic sleeve. As soon as she'd seen numbers, she'd folded it over as if it were indeed garbage. "My earring doesn't seem to be here. Thanks so much for your help, Chuck."

"May I see that?" It didn't sound like a question.

She quickly unfolded the plastic sleeve and closed it again. "Headed for the garbage. Enjoy the evening. I think I'll take my husband's advice and read a book."

A couple of minutes ago, he might have paid attention to the husband comment. Now, he was focused on the paper. "Is that what you were really looking for?"

"I had no idea this was in here," she said with indignation. This much was true. "Plastic does not belong in compost. This is clearly garbage and has to be removed. Plastic can take between 20 and 500 years to decompose, and the folks here surely don't want pieces of plastic in their vegetable beds! And plastics degrade into microplastics, which can affect the food web, and pollute groundwater, among other problems..."

"Enough, already! They told me to report anything out of the ordinary. What are those numbers on that paper?"

"Who's they?"

"The people who hired me."

"I thought you said Hank Archer hired you."

"I don't have to answer your questions, ma'am. You should give me that paper."

"And I don't have to obey you about anything except my own security here."

She walked off in a huff and felt his eyes following her. *Who is he going to call? I hope I have some time here.*

As she climbed the stairs, she heard him resetting the alarm.

Back in her room, she locked the door. And the windows, for good measure. She drew the curtains. She washed her gloves and left them on, and then got a washcloth and removed tomato and Lord knows what else from the plastic casing.

The paper was marked "CONFIDENTIAL."

She called Ted Nguyen and left a message. "I've found something that may be important to the case. Please call me back ASAP."

The numbers seemed to be related to the Garden's endowment fund. It was a document from a brokerage firm, showing a beginning balance of well over ten million dollars. There were two dates within the last month when the amount shrank. Significantly. The first stock sale was three weeks earlier. It was for about 500k. The second was close to three million.

And there was a note, in the margin, written in the careful cursive that she'd read on the Post-it in the banana slug file. It was dated three days ago, the day before they'd all arrived in La Jolla for the weekend. "Talked to Hank about this. Says he's checking into it, seemed surprised—but not as shocked as he should be. Told me not to do anything about it until he's 'done some looking.' Wondering if I should call an emergency board meeting, if Hank doesn't have something to say by Monday at noon. If he does, we should both call one! Will check with brokerage on Monday AM. Discuss with Bea."

Bea would do some of her own looking, damn it.

She took a photo of the document and sent it to Ted Nguyen.

CHAPTER FIFTEEN

It was time to do more internet research. As Bea opened her laptop, she decided that Hank Archer was the obvious person to start with. She had looked him up earlier and found his social connections. She'd have to dig deeper. Also, maybe she could find something out about whoever else might have hired Chuck Fox.

She settled into the heavy oak desk set that faced a wall full of seabird photographs. Like everything in her large bedroom, it was perfectly placed. No *real* ocean views to distract from work.

Hank had spent most of his life as CEO of Archer and Associates, a commercial real estate leasing and sales company doing business throughout southern California. There weren't any stories about malfeasance, for whatever that was worth. In the last couple of years, he had gone into biotech, which was a hot industry in San Diego, providing venture capital funds to a small start-up working on brain cancer treatment. She found the boards of directors of both groups. Arthur, Max, and Lester Pearson —Paige's father?—were on the biotech start-up board.

She could dig deeper into Hank's business or look into a couple of the other folks. Arthur Blakely, Hank's companion on the foggy overlook a few hours earlier, was a complete unknown. Why not start with him?

A quick search revealed that Blakely was the CEO of one of San Diego's largest public relations firms and a close friend of one of San Diego's influential city councilmen. His company, Blakely and Associates, had worked with many of the city's largest businesses, especially in the tech and biotech industries.

Paige's parents, the Pearsons, weren't on the La Jolla Gardens board, but they were unseen players in this whole drama. If Camila was right, they were lobbying behind the scenes against her. And they were certainly old friends of the founders and other La Jollans. Surely they wouldn't be involved in their daughter's murder, but it didn't hurt to look them up. She didn't know their first names, but she found them easily enough when she googled Paige. Lester Pearson owned high-end hotels in San Diego and Orange Counties. Marge Pearson had her own clothing line which was available only in "luxury" shopping locations.

They were all fine, upstanding, philanthropically inclined citizens, at least they seemed to be from what Bea had been able to find in the last hour.

She sighed and sat quietly for a moment, listening. A distant motorcycle, a couple of squawks from the aviary, a bit of a breeze waving the palm trees. She put her head down and looked up Max Danes, that charming white-haired man with a cane, the one who'd come to dinner the first night. Hank had said Max would be joining the board in a couple of months.

Max Danes had started his own insurance company as a young man and was currently CEO of one of the largest independent insurance agencies in southern California. He had a new venture, Magickal Nature, a supplements company. Interestingly, the company had lost a class-action lawsuit that claimed that unlabeled stimulants had been added to Vitaliti, a supposedly herbal remedy to "boost energy and focus." She checked out the FDA web site and found a warning letter about Vitaliti.

Hank Archer was on the board of Magickal Nature.

The company had paid $3.3 million in fines, but it was still in business.

She'd better communicate this right away.

Bea called Ted Nguyen again and got voice mail. She left a message that she had some concrete information related to the case, which she had discovered in a compost bin. She said she was feeling uneasy about the garden's new security guard, who wanted to take the document from her, and was going to "call the people who hired him" ASAP. The document indicated that there had been huge withdrawals from the Gardens' endowment fund. Both Max Danes and Hank Archer were on the board of Magickal Nature, a company that had just had to pay 3.3 million dollars for malfeasance.

It didn't really make sense to call 911, but... Allie had handed her a business card. Bea's hand shot into her pants pocket and drew out the card.

Maybe she was being paranoid. But people had been getting hurt and killed. She rang Allie, who she hoped was diligently watching the house. *I feel like I can trust her. I hope I'm not wrong about this. I trust her more than Chuck Fox, for sure.*

"Allie Chung." Her voice was reassuringly calm.

"Allie, I can't reach Ted Nguyen. And I believe I've found something important to the case. Chuck Fox knows I found it, and he said he had to 'call the board members who hired me' about it. I don't think Fox really saw what was on the... paper. But, you know, some of the La Jolla Gardens board members may be on the suspect list for what happened to Paige, and the others, and well... you yourself warned me about power brokers in La Jolla. Somebody else did, too."

"Slow down. What do you want me to do?"

"Well, if you can't reach Nguyen, maybe try somebody else at the San Diego Police Department? They might listen to a security guard. And please watch to see if anybody tries to come in."

"You're all locked in tight, in your room, right?"

"Yes, and Chuck Fox set the alarm for the outside doors. But he might let in one of the board members he mentioned. I don't know if he has a key to my room."

"Okay, Bea. I'm on it."

Bea ended the call. She sat in her desk chair, staring at the phone she'd put down, unable to decide what to do next. Should she warn Lila? She decided to text her a picture of the suspicious document, with some explanation. Good thing she'd splurged on a phone that took pictures; this was the third time she'd used this tool today. She checked the picture she'd taken of Chuck Fox. He looked more gangster than cop. His bulging muscles now seemed more threatening than reassuring. *It's amazing how my feelings about someone can affect their appearance.*

She started to put the incriminating paper away in her desk drawer. *That's way too easy for anyone to find.* She looked around the room. She ended up wrapping the paper in its plastic sleeve inside her old UC Santa Cruz nightshirt and tucked it into the bottom of her suitcase. The hiding place seemed a fitting tribute to Paige.

Now what? Lila hadn't responded to the text. Bea slipped out of her room and tried Lila's door. It was locked, of course. She walked quickly back into her own room and locked her door again. She called Lila but it went to voice mail. She'd probably fallen asleep watching her stupidly funny movie.

Maybe Bea should find a light novel on her Kindle, as Frank had suggested. But even that required too much concentration. She picked a book off the guest room shelf. *Famous Crimes in La Jolla.* She couldn't get away from it. Right next to *Famous Homes of La Jolla.* She looked at the latter, found "Archer" in the index, and looked at the house. She thought she recognized the boxwood hedge and the gate with a huge golden "A" on it. Just a few houses down. Well, maybe Hank Archer was in the *Crimes of La Jolla* index, too. She checked and thank God he wasn't.

Max Danes wasn't in either book. Maybe his home wasn't famous. Or maybe he didn't live in La Jolla, although she'd seen earlier that he was on the board of the local country club. Or maybe he was a very private person. Not everybody wanted their front entrance publicized.

Were these the people Allie Chung had checked on, and said there hadn't been a light on in their homes all night?

This was useless.

She sank into the pillowy armchair but got right up. She wanted her senses fine-tuned. She pulled her phone out of her pocket... maybe she'd turned it off by mistake. She hadn't and there were no messages. Running her hands through her hair, she looked at the books she'd already downloaded on her Kindle. She couldn't concentrate on any of them. She paced across the room and came back to her computer. There was no avoiding it. She could at least pretend like she was moving this mystery forward.

She searched for Charles Fox on her computer, but stopped hammering at the keyboard when she thought she heard a car pull up out front. She wished she had a deadbolt, but this wasn't a hotel room. Peering through the keyhole was pointless. Bea slowly turned the lock on the doorknob.

From the hallway, she could look down to the living room windows on the ground floor. The SafeT car was slowly monitoring the driveway loop. At least she hoped that's what it was doing. She went back inside her bedroom, shut the door, locked it and returned to her computer.

There were a lot of Charles Foxes, and none of the information was particularly helpful. Should she really be trusting Allie Chung? She was mostly relying on intuition.

There was an Allison Chung who'd been valedictorian at a southside high school a couple of years ago. The girl in the local newspaper picture looked like the security guard in La Jolla. Why wasn't she at a prestigious college, with that background? This puzzle was almost enough to divert Bea's attention from her hypervigilant listening.

She heard something at the back of the house. She held her breath and stilled her hands. A door back there opened, and somebody dropped something and cursed. Was that Chuck's voice? She heard four dings... he must be disarming the security system. He was walking across the house to the living room. The front door, probably. A bolt clicked. She wasn't moving even an eyelash.

Another voice, coming from the front door. "Where's Bea?" It sounded like Hank. She was surprised his tone was so mild and everyday, given the situation. She imagined Fox pointing up to her bedroom.

Then there were two heavy footfalls on the stairs, one a lot faster than the other. Her hand was on her phone, calling 911, when someone unlocked her bedroom door. Chuck Fox. He must have had a master key! His look was cold enough to give her goosebumps. His hand was quite close to the gun in his waistband.

Hank came up behind him, frowning. "Whoa there, Chuck. Why didn't you knock?" He placed a hand on Chuck's shoulder, but Chuck shook it off. "Take it easy, buddy. Bea, you look frightened. I'm sorry to scare you. Let's sit down and talk, if you don't mind, Bea." Hank was almost cordial.

Bea wasn't feeling a bit cordial.

"Keep the door open." She said it loudly, so Lila could hear, if she woke up.

Bea was dimly aware that somebody else had come into the house, through the front door. *Please let it be the police.*

"Bea, you ok?" a female voice shouted from somewhere downstairs. It sounded like Allie.

"Not sure. Please come up here," Bea yelled as loudly

as her voice box would let her. *That would wake Lila up.*

"Shut up," Fox said.

How could I not have seen right away what a total jerk he is?

Running footsteps on the stairs. Hank had taken a seat at her desk and motioned her towards the big, pillowy armchair. He shrugged his shoulders.

"This is really unnecessary..." He was still acting as if this were a normal social occasion.

"It's absolutely necessary when two men burst into your room. Especially when our little weekend gathering has had two likely murders and one possible attempted murder," Bea told him.

Allie came in with her gun drawn, with Lila behind her. Bea jerked her head at Lila, motioning for her to stay out of the room.

Lila disappeared as Chuck Fox drew his gun.

"Put your guns away for Pete's sake!' Hank shouted. "I'd like to have a civilized conversation here. Who the hell are you?" he said to Allie.

She's a superhero in a white polyester uniform shirt and cargo pants.

"Allison Chung. I'm the neighborhood security guard. I'm in touch with Detective Nguyen, who asked me to keep an eye on comings and goings here."

"I see. Well, Ms. Whatever-Your-Name-Is, you're welcome to stay."

Allie looked at Bea, her eyebrows raised. Bea nodded at her and turned to Hank. "If you're serious about having a civilized conversation, you need to tell Mr. Fox to leave. He can go back outdoors to patrol."

"Do that," Hank said. Chuck Fox looked most unwilling, but he holstered his weapon and left the room anyway, casting a questioning glance at Hank, who didn't respond. Hank looked at Bea, instead. "I'm a reasonable man, Bea."

Allie was watching Hank closely. She turned to Bea for a moment and gave her a thumbs-up. *A thumbs-up? Really?*

Hank said in a conversational tone. "Now then, Bea, our impetuous young security guard, Mr. Fox, tells me that you found a garden document with figures on it in the compost bin, of all places. I live almost next door, and I thought I'd come and talk to you about it. I won't see you before you leave, otherwise. And I'm busy in the morning. As president and treasurer, I should know if an important document has been thrown away."

"I think the police should see it," Bea said.

Hank's reply was interrupted by noise downstairs. Several people were coming in the front door.

"Who the hell is that?" Hank asked. He *seemed* to be sincerely surprised, but who knew. At any rate, more people were bounding up the stairs. Allie went to the door and pointed her gun at whoever was running up the stairs. "Stop right there," she demanded.

"Let's not have any gunfire. We can do this in a civilized way," said an older man's voice from the hallway.

These "civilized" people give the word a whole new meaning. Bea started looking around for something to crouch behind. The room was already crowded...

Chuck was back at the door. With his gun drawn, and with another rough-looking character also with a drawn gun.

"Stand aside, madam." Bea recognized the older man's voice just as he materialized behind his two henchmen.

"Max!" Hank shouted. "What the hell are *you* doing here?"

"Same thing you are, I imagine," Max panted from his climb up the stairs and leaned heavily on his cane. Shooting a smile at Hank, he said, in his light, shaky voice, "Chuck alerted both of us."

"For God's sake, Max, call them off! We were having a calm conversation. I'm sure Bea will be happy to let me, as president and treasurer, have the document. You're not even on the board yet, and you shouldn't be here, especially with these... people."

I shouldn't be here, either. I can't run; they're blocking the door and they have guns. Her pounding heart must be audible to everyone.

Max seemed completely comfortable in this horrible situation. "Well, Hank, I will be on the board, soon, and I was with you when we hired Chuck here. Of course, we'd met before," he added with a chuckle. "I did have a little something to do with his current employment."

Hank's tan skin went chalky, but he said nothing as Max continued, "I gave him my card and told him to call both of us if anything unusual came up tonight. And it has." He advanced between the three armed men and put an imperious hand out to Bea. She did not make a comment about kissing his ring, a comment that seemed to belong to a different Bea in a different world. This was real. This was terrifying. She might actually die over an investment firm document. It would be absurd if it weren't so scary she could barely breathe.

"Give it to me," he commanded. "Please," he added, in a nod to his upbringing and class.

Well, I have the picture on my phone. And Nguyen has the copy I sent to him. "Okay," Bea said. She swallowed and walked to her suitcase, followed by Fox. She unwrapped her nightshirt and pulled the document out. Her hands were so sweaty they stuck to the plastic-covered paper.

Despite his cane, Max had made it to her side unbelievably quickly. He snatched the paper from her. "That's the ticket, Bea. Now these gentlemen will be happy to escort you out."

"Out where? To Tijuana?" Bea asked, finding a voice that was stronger than she felt.

"Watch it, Miss Rivers," Max said, with a smile that did not conceal his ill will. His gentlemanly breeding was like artwork that masks an entirely different underpainting. Bea's fears raced ahead of her reason. *This guy thinks he can do whatever he wants. And by God, maybe he can.* Chuck jabbed a gun into her back. He made sure it hurt. "Lila!" Bea yelled. *But what could Lila do? I'll just get her into this mess. She could call 911, maybe.*

"Hang, on, Bea. We don't need you, Lila!" Allie called out, as the other thug put a gun to her back. Allie seemed remarkably calm, even when told to drop the gun and put her hands up.

"Nobody wants violence here," Max said, gesturing with his chin to Bea and Allie. *But maybe you want violence elsewhere?*

As if she'd voiced her question, he said, "You two can take a little trip to the ocean with me and my colleagues. Desert dwellers seem to enjoy the ocean, although they're notoriously bad swimmers." He laughed at Bea's gasp. She was suddenly wet with sweat.

"That's quite enough," said a new, stern voice. Bea hadn't heard anyone else approaching.

Detective Nguyen! Finally! With Detective Bingham and another officer. They maneuvered quickly into safe positions, covering Chuck and Max's thugs. Nguyen was pointing his gun at Max. They must have crept up the stairs while everyone was preoccupied.

"Drop your weapons. Hands up. Ms. Chung, please secure their weapons." Allie picked her own gun off the floor, holstered it, and leaned to scoop up the other guns. Chuck Fox kicked his away. It landed near Bea, who kicked it towards Allie.

Chuck called Bea an epithet so squalid she might have been shocked, but there was no space left in the shocked area in her brain. Allie secured the guns, making sure the safety was on for each one. She emptied the chambers, put the bullets in one pocket, stuck two guns in her waistband, and put the last one in another pocket of her cargo pants.

Bea was breathing hard.

The three police officers had held the guns steady. "Now proceed slowly to the floor," Detective Nguyen commanded. "Heads down, lie on your stomachs. Hands behind your backs." Bea shook her head to clear the improbable image she was seeing, but it was still there. A room crowded with two cops and a security guard, armed. Max, Hank and Chuck and some unknown thugs lying on the floor.

Nguyen and the two other officers quicky handcuffed the five on the floor.

Allie said, "I got everything they just said on tape." She waved a tiny digital recorder at the officers.

"Good job. And thank you for the 911 call, Lila, although we were on the way," he said, as Lila appeared in the doorway. Max Danes, you are under arrest for the murder of Paige Pearson and Ace Karlsson. You have the right to remain silent..."

The rest of them were arrested, too... and told the charges were yet to be determined. "There are plenty of serious charges to choose from," Nguyen said.

"You are making a serious mistake. I was having a polite conversation with Bea here when these others came barging in with guns!" Hank yelled. His face had turned reddish purple.

"You'll have the opportunity to explain all this down at the station," Nguyen said.

"We were going to pay it back!" Hank sputtered.

"Shut up," Max said to his colleague." He turned his head towards Nguyen. And you... you'll regret this," he snarled. "I have a very good lawyer."

"I'm quite sure you do," Nguyen said, with a smile.

CHAPTER SIXTEEN

By sunrise, Bea had roused Lila and they were sipping coffee in the living room. Bea hadn't been able to find any large mugs, so they were making do with small, flowered cups and saucers with "made in Italy" painted on the bottom. Bea had made the brew double strength, and she thought she'd still need three cups. She'd been far too tense to sleep. They'd found some leftover papaya and toast, which they'd managed to burn. After putting new slices in the toaster, and paying attention to the settings, they were trying to decide if they wanted to take a last walk on the beach before they left at 10:00 to catch a 1:00 flight (Lila was against it) when the doorbell rang.

"For God's sake, now what?" Bea asked. Once again, they looked through the peephole in the door to see who it was. *Margaret.* Bea opened the door.

"Bea, dear, I wanted to catch you before you left, since I won't be home for another week. The Pearsons called me last night about the arrests. I just can't believe it," Margaret said. She hadn't bothered with makeup, and her hair wasn't sprayed down, for once. She looked as rumpled as Bea felt.

"Margaret, let's sit down and talk about this."

They sank into the cushions, Bea and Lila on the couch together, Margaret in an armchair.

"No one in this neighborhood is going to believe it. These men are pillars of our community. I feel... bad... that I pointed you towards Camila. And Armando, of course. The odd thing is, we all thought Max had plenty of money to cover business losses. That he would embezzle it from a nonprofit! It's just unthinkable. His wife is *stricken.* And poor dear Melanie Archer. It's mortifying for her."

"I imagine so," Bea said in her best deadpan. She was sure that Detective Nguyen would figure out if Melanie was in on Hank's plans. She'd been cool towards her husband about *something* when they'd had lunch. Bea had thought it was his randiness, but maybe Melanie had been angry with him about embezzling. Or at getting caught at it.

"Of course, I'm sure they meant to pay it back," Margaret said, interrupting her musing.

"Of course," Lila said, imitating Bea's tone.

"My dear Charles *did* say... well, I really shouldn't say."

But she clearly wanted to. This was interesting. "What did he say?' Bea asked, affecting nonchalance as she leaned over to put a little more milk in her coffee.

"Well, he accused Max of cheating at tennis. You know, calling shots out when they were inside, but he missed them. But that's a little thing. He's been so *successful* at everything he does. Hank, too."

"Then they had no reason to think they couldn't be successful with this scheme," Bea said.

"I suppose you're right. It's given me a lot to think about. My Charles *did* say you could tell a lot about a man by the way he played tennis. Well, and golf. They kind of changed to golf in their later years..."

"I'm not surprised either one of them cheated at sports," Bea said. "You told me to beware of people in this neighborhood who have money and power. I didn't expect one to hire thugs to stick a gun in my back, though." Bea said that last sentence angrily enough that Margaret drew back.

"He did *that?* Oh, Bea, I *am* sorry."

"I can tell you are. But I'm fine. Paige and Ace and Armando are not fine."

"Yes, I… it's just so dreadful that I can't quite picture it. Max paid Ace to push her off the cliff?"

"That's what it looks like to me, Margaret. I guess we'll find out more in time. I was thinking somebody could have sneaked in by a back route but Ace didn't have to sneak anywhere. I suspect Max also paid some guy to kill Ace and take his payoff back."

"You mean *Max* hired some Mexican criminal to kill that young man? Oh, surely not!"

"I'm sure he'll get a fair trial."

"With excellent attorneys," Lila added.

"I suspect Max also paid some woman to tie Armando into his sling the wrong way, too. But I did notice that Detective Nguyen didn't mention Armando when he told Max he was under arrest."

Margaret sucked in a breath and let it out. "But why in the world would Max want Armando killed?"

"Well, I have a theory. Because the women on the board wanted him to be the executive director, and Max knew Armando wasn't the kind of patsy he wanted in that job. Paige grew up around Max and his ilk and had some reservations about upsetting the apple carts of her parents' friends… like you. If Paige was thinking of going to the police about the missing endowment funds, once she was gone, Armando for sure wouldn't do Max's bidding as executive director. Max would have to find a true loyalist. As we know, Armando loves upsetting apple carts."

Margaret nodded, but there was doubt in her eyes.

Bea continued with her theory. "As a board member, he probably would have gone along with the two women on most things, and Hank wanted a contingent that not only wouldn't question his financial actions but would also agree on those issues about no more native plants, water use… that kind of thing."

Margaret sighed and shook her head. She pivoted to discussion of one of her crowd she felt certain was a good guy. "Well, at least Arthur is a fine man. The Pearsons called him first. He's horrified about the arrests."

"And about what they did?"

"Yes, of course, although I don't know if the Pearsons gave him all the... details. I expect he'll be interim board president. Heaven knows what they'll do about an executive director."

"You told me Samira is the VP. Wouldn't she become president?"

"Oh, dear. I suppose so."

Bea and Lila exchanged a look. "We have to get ready to go to the airport," Bea said.

"Oh. Of course. You ladies have a good trip. I'll see you in Tucson." Margaret collected her pocketbook and her tattered dignity and went out the door. Her hand shook on the door handle.

When the door had shut behind her, Lila said, "I prefer my board member. She's quite a lot more clear-eyed."

"Well, yes. But Margaret's world is upended. Who knows how that will affect her?"

"Good luck with that."

They collected their roller bags from their rooms. Bea said a mental farewell to the waves and the surfers. *It's too bad my positive memories of this place have been erased by that terrifying scene.* Bea and Lila waited for a cab, which arrived an hour later, and they got into it in thick fog.

"Cold," Lila observed.

"Yes, but we could use some of this in a couple of months," Bea said. They didn't discuss the events of the weekend in their cab. Fortunately, that seemed fine with the grumpy older driver, who clearly was not doing this for pocket change while he studied at UCSD or went out on the town. And fortunately, he didn't seem to realize that he was picking them up at what would probably become a locally famous location. Not in a good way.

There were about six people gawking at the boxwood

hedge with the "A" on the golden gate. A TV live remote truck pulled up as they sped by. Bea and Lila exchanged a silent look.

They kept their counsel about the murders until Bea's phone rang in the waiting area for the flight. It was an unfamiliar number with an 858 prefix, which Bea had learned was north San Diego County.

She took the call as she walked the concourse, moving quickly so that no one could track the conversation.

"Bea," said a tentative woman's voice. "It's Samira Singh. We met at the door to the Gardens yesterday."

"I remember."

"First of all, thank you for your part in finding the murderers. I guess I should say the murderer and his accomplices and the embezzler."

"All I did was find a piece of paper."

"A very incriminating piece of paper, I hear. And you sent a photo of that new security guard to the police. He has quite a record. Under another name, of course. Believe me, we won't be using that company anymore. And now I find that you also sent a copy of that document to the police, as well. You sped things up considerably. On behalf of the board, thank you. And I'm terribly sorry you were in such danger."

"It's over now. I'm sure ready to be home."

"That's understandable. This is a long shot, but do you think your job would give you release time to direct our garden until we hire someone?"

"Samira, I'm honored you asked me. But I have my hands full in Tucson. I don't have anybody ready to sub for me if I take a leave of absence, and more importantly, I've got a husband and two young kids there. But... if you need advice with the hiring process, I could help."

Samira sighed. It was a prolonged sigh, as if she had to let all the air—heavily polluted air—out of her lungs.

"Guess I have to do it, then. May I call you for if we

have questions as we move along?"

"Sure. And there are resources available to you. I can help you with that, and..." She stopped for a moment, and then said, "They're calling our plane. I have to go, but thank you, Samira. I'm sure the garden's in good hands."

"I wish I had more than two of them."

"Oh... and Samira? Would you let me know the details of Paige's memorial service? I'd like to attend."

"I gather you were good friends. I'm so sorry for your loss."

"Well, we weren't close friends. But she was a colleague and we knew each other in college. I was hoping to get to know her better this weekend, actually. I wish I could have done something to prevent what happened." She wouldn't go into banana slugs. "I really have to go. But I'm sure the garden will do well with you as the head!"

Bea and Lila got settled in their seats on the plane, Lila having remembered to check in right away this time; Bea didn't have to save her a seat. After taking off, the plane swooped out above the Pacific, and then turned inland over downtown with its skyscrapers and houses on tiny lots running up and down the hills. Bea caught a glimpse of the tall, beige sandstone cliffs of La Jolla north of town and just within her sight lines. She was glad she'd be back for the memorial service. Maybe next time she could leave this beautiful place with more peace in her soul. She'd seen enough guns for the rest of her life.

An hour later, the plane descended into brown hills that were seas of yellow, up close. The palo verde trees had gone from nearly full bloom to all-out glory. She wanted OUT of the plane. Someone's overhead bag spilled pill bottles all over the floor, and they had to scoop everything up before anyone could go by.

After what seemed like an hour, but was probably about twenty minutes, Bea and Lila got to the baggage claim. And there they were... Frank, Andy and Jessie.

Jessie leapt into her arms, and Frank gathered up Andy for a four-way hug. "Frank took us out of school early!" Jessie shrieked into Bea's ear. Frank brushed Bea's hair out of her eyes and kissed an eyebrow. "I'm so damned glad to see you safely in Tucson. Honey, you have to be tired. Let's get you home!"

"Not tired. Totally exhausted." She kissed him hard, ruffled Andy's carrot top, brushed her lips across the top of Jessie's head. "Now I'm only somewhat exhausted."

She suddenly registered that Lila was standing off to the side. She put her daughter down. "Andy and Jessie, you remember Lila, don't you? From Copperton?"

"Yeah, she makes really good hot chocolate," Andy said, nodding his head vigorously.

Lila stepped forward. "That's a good thing to be known for. And you must be Frank. Delighted to meet you. Thanks for letting me crash with you. It's just too much to drive to Copperton tonight. And I have to go to that famous supermarket of yours before I head back! I can't live without their giant chocolate bars and aged Gouda cheese and I have a list from a couple of others from Copperton, too."

Frank touched her arm. "I'm very glad you're here. Maybe you can help me make sense of what little I've gleaned from Bea about your godawful weekend."

"Why was it godawful, Mom?" Andy asked. He was a worrier, and he'd gotten bullied by classmates about his mother's working at a place with two murders. Bea and Frank weren't about to discuss what Bea was calling The Events of the Weekend with the kids.

"Ah, dry air!" Lila exclaimed in the crosswalk to the parking garage.

"Not much of a coastal type, Lila?" Frank asked.

"Give me the desert every time."

"Even when the heat kicks in big time?"

"Even then."

CHAPTER SEVENTEEN

Bea was sitting on the patio in their ranch-style Tucson home two days after Lila had gone back to Copperton. Her neighborhood was infinitely more modest than the one she'd just visited, but she had far more privacy than any director would ever have in that mansion.

She sank into the camp chair that doubled as patio furniture and watched a bat hovering by an agave flower high above her head. The small miracle of pollination. Her life felt rich in small miracles. One of them was in the kitchen seeking wine.

The kids were in bed, and they could finally discuss more than the bare bones of the momentous events of the weekend. Bea had gotten some more information that day.

Solar lights shone on the base of the big, spreading mesquite that provided shade during the day. Its yellow blooms were not so bright or spectacular as the palo verde's, but Bea was glad to see them as she aimed her flashlight beam at the blossoms.

Frank arrived from the kitchen with a wooden tray containing a very good bottle of cabernet and their two best wine glasses, fragile balloon ones that sat in the cabinet for a year at a time. "We deserve this," he said, as he slowly poured two glasses, and handed her one.

Bea jumped up to embrace him, nearly spilling their precious wine. She'd been impulsive and weepy ever since she got back. She might have met Ace's fate in Tijuana, never holding Frank again, never watching her kids grow up... She marveled at all the people in the world who'd survived worse disasters, in mass shootings, and in wars. How did they remain their old stable selves? Many didn't. She would, she hoped. The bad dreams would taper off.

"Frank, I heard from Allie Chung. I want you to meet her when we go back for Paige's memorial."

"I'd like to get a look at all of these characters."

"Allie is going to get a job with the San Diego Police Department," Bea said. "Ted Nguyen was really pleased with her work. She told me she's been working three jobs to support her younger brothers and sisters, and she could go to school while she makes enough money with the San Diego Police Department. She's over the moon with the possibility. She was high school valedictorian. I'm so glad for her."

Frank gave her a sidelong look. "Nguyen will probably offer you something, too, Ms. Sleuth."

Bea raised an eyebrow. "Well, Frank, I do believe I'll pass up any career opportunities that open up. Including the directorship of La Jolla Gardens."

"That's a relief."

"Lila called today, too."

"How's she doing?"

"She's not having nightmares. But she said *she'd* pass up the next offer of a beach house in La Jolla. She's happy to be around people who have a more modest opinion of their own power and privilege than that crowd. She said she'd never complain about her board members again."

"Entirely reasonable. But do take up an offer of a beach house if we get one."

She squeezed his hand.

"Lila also reported that Gert said she'd learned a lot at the meeting. She doesn't want to expand the board, ever, in case they get a 'bunch of crackpots like they have in La Jolla.' She thinks three people is just fine. And she thinks they should keep rich folks off, so 'there's no hanky-panky.' That's Gert's takeaway."

They laughed and sipped some more wine.

"So clear a few things up for me, Bea. Hank didn't know that Max had hired these goons... which may not be fair to Ace, from what you say... and Hank didn't know that Max had shelled out all kinds of cash for hired killers to protect the secret of their embezzlement?"

"He said he didn't. He stared at Max with what looked to me like horror and incomprehension as they were hauled off. He said, 'But we were going to pay it back!' And no, I wouldn't call Ace a goon. He was one of those kids who's always been unpopular, and he found a fringe political group online that accepted him. He figured he could be a hero if he presented them with all that money... which of course Max had an actual goon steal off of Ace's dead body in Tijuana. Max probably saw Ace as a good investment, not an actual person."

"No doubt."

"So anyway, Detective Nguyen and a Mexican detective found the killer and got a confession out of him. I guess that's what Nguyen was doing when we couldn't reach him for a while."

"That must have been so unnerving."

The phone rang at this point. Bea checked the number. "My God, it's Margaret! I wonder what she wants!"

Frank nodded to her to take the call. She put it on speakerphone and told Margaret she was doing so.

"Fine, of course. Bea, dear, I wanted to call you with some news. I've just had cocktails with the Pearsons, and of course they are up to date on everything with the case. Or I guess I should say 'the cases.' It'll all be in the San Diego paper in the morning. You were right about everything you guessed. Except for Armando."

"Armando?"

"Yes, his Lothario lifestyle got him in trouble. It had nothing to do with La Jolla Gardens! But La Jolla will be agog. Again."

"Please don't keep me in suspense."

"Well, he was having an affair with a young woman that my friends all know. You've never met her. Anyway, she's married to an older man we know even better. She asked him for a divorce, based upon Armando's professions of undying commitment, or whatever, and lo and behold, the commitment was a little wishy-washy. An old story. So, this woman hired another woman to loosen Armando's safety straps. The one at the Gliderport has confessed."

"Looks like somebody else bought themselves a murder. I'll bet it cost a mint… but fortunately, this was only an attempted one."

"Well now Bea, maybe she only wanted to hurt him. Shake him up."

"Maybe. I certainly don't know." Bea sucked in a breath. "I keep suspecting Armando every time there's a murder. I clearly have prejudices."

"Like everybody else on Earth," Frank interjected from the sidelines. "I have no fondness for that man, Margaret."

"Nor I," Margaret said. "But I've been quite fond of Hank, and I've known Max forever. I find it so hard to believe that Max hired Ace to *kill* that lovely girl, whom I've known her whole life."

"Hank must have told him he'd talked to Paige about the withdrawals," Bea said."

"And then Max killed Ace, getting rid of the evidence, and recouping his money," Frank added.

"Yes, well, that, too. I haven't been able to even *think* about that part."

"It's been pretty tough for all of us, in different ways," Bea said.

"I'm so horrified that someone actually trained a gun on you."

"That was only a part of what Max had in mind. But Frank and I were just about to enjoy a glass of wine together. I'll see you at the committee meeting on Friday! Thanks for updating me, Margaret."

"Have a good evening, Bea dear."

"That woman's worldview is cracking at the seams," Frank observed, when Bea had hung up.

"I'm going to assume it'll make her a better board member." Bea took a sip of wine. "Frank, this is wonderful!"

"The cost was wondrous, as well."

"A wondrous bargain?"

"Nope." He took a sip and closed his eyes. They sat quietly for a few moments.

"Armando was definitely traveling in well-heeled circles over there," he said.

"Unlike his time in Tucson, where he was just an assistant professor seeking tenure."

"That guy. Well, he got more than he bargained for with this recent love affair."

Bea took another sip of wine. "I wonder if Samira and Maria will still want him on the board. Maybe they'll ask me about him as a board member. I don't really think it's appropriate for me to mention his time on my board unless they ask. But it must be on his curriculum vitae." She sighed again. "Actually, I'm sure those two women will do fine. Even with that Arthur Blakely guy still on the board."

"You don't know Blakely. He could be a straight arrow."

"True. Fair enough. I've gotten awfully suspicious. I even suspected Margaret for a moment. And Camila. I feel terrible about that. She's had enough pain and prejudice in her life without being accused of murdering the elite of La Jolla," Bea said.

"Yeah. I can see why she could have been a suspect when it was just Paige that got killed, but from the way you describe her, I don't see her murdering Ace in Tijuana. I hope she can go to law school."

"Agreed." Bea said.

They were silent for a few moments. A barn owl hooted quite close by, maybe in the neighbors' Aleppo pine. A couple of bats swooped under the garage light. A motorcycle made its noisy way down the alley behind the house.

"We're all glad you're back in one piece, Bea," Frank said. "I'm sure Angus is, too."

"Yes, his attitude towards administration is to ignore everything until I get back. People have to find him on the grounds to ask a question; he ignores voice mail and email more than usual when he's temporarily in charge. I still haven't made it through all the messages he ignored while I was gone." She sighed. "But I have to say it feels good to be back at work. At this time of year, it's a daily pleasure to see what's come into bloom..."

"Let's have your parents over for dinner tomorrow before they go back to California."

"Yes." She rubbed her forehead. "I guess Dad still hasn't gotten his test results back."

"But your mother's worried it's serious. He's sure lost a lot of weight."

"*That* is the kind of thing I should be worrying about, that and Andy's latest run-in with this dad."

"If you had to do it over again, would you have stayed out of the fray in La Jolla?"

Bea looked at Frank. "Probably not," he answered for her.

"Well, let's hope that sort of question never comes up again," Bea said.

Her husband seemed to find that quite amusing.

Acknowledgements

Like some of the other characters in this book, I am fundamentally a Southwesterner. I also love the ocean and wanted to write a mystery set on the foggy southern California coast. The unpleasant and unprincipled La Jolla residents in this book do not reflect the many wonderful people I know from this area, but when you write a mystery, there do need to be several plausible suspects!

I'm grateful to so many who've helped with this book. My publisher/editor, Geoff Habiger of Artemesia Publishing, continues to show great patience and insight. Bill Singleton went through many iterations of the lovely cover design until we got it just right, yet again. My Women Writing the West mystery group, composed of Laura Alderson, Betsy Randolph, and Mary Coley, has been invaluable. Thank goodness that Betsy has law enforcement experience and could help with those details. Margaret Harmon and Betty Spence made detailed beta readings that improved things immensely. And my husband Phil listens, suggests, and does whatever is most helpful in our lives so that I can write.

I dedicated the book to deserts and oceans, and I want to acknowledge how critical both have been to my life, happiness, and urge to write.

About the Author

Marty Eberhardt is a retired botanical garden executive director and nonprofit professional who now delights in using the right side of her brain to write fiction. *Death in a Desert Garden*, her first novel, won the Arizona/ New Mexico Book Award for cozy mystery in 2022, two Firebird awards, and the bronze CIPA/EVVY award for cozy mystery. *Bones in the Back Forty*, the second in the Bea Rivers botanical garden mystery, won the 2025 New Mexico Book Award for cozy mystery and two Firebird awards, and was an *Albuquerque Journal* "Book of the Week." Marty and her husband divide their time between Tucson and the small mountain town of Silver City, NM, enjoying the enjoying the flora, fauna, wild areas and wild characters of both.